英語力 Starter

16堂流利英語聽說入門訓練課

English Now—Starter: Listening and Speaking in Everyday Life

作者 Owain Mckimm 譯者 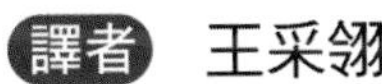

審訂 Helen Yeh

如何下載 MP3 音檔

❶ 寂天雲 APP 聆聽：掃描書上 QR Code 下載「寂天雲 - 英日語學習隨身聽」APP。加入會員後，用 APP 內建掃描器再次掃描書上 QR Code，即可使用 APP 聆聽音檔。

❷ 官網下載音檔：請上「寂天閱讀網」（www.icosmos.com.tw），註冊會員／登入後，搜尋本書，進入本書頁面，點選「MP3 下載」下載音檔，存於電腦等其他播放器聆聽使用。

Introduction

本書是一本專為初級英語學習者撰寫的書籍，強調學生英語**口語**與**聽力**的養成。全書分為16個與日常息息相關的主題單元，每單元含豐富活動，除有單字配對、聽力練習等，為口說能力打下扎實基礎，另外還有雙人對話模擬練習、替換詞組練習、開放式回答練習等，引導學生藉由模仿、重複，將內容轉化為自發口說。

本書不特別講解文法，也不強調解題，而是藉由多樣的活動，幫助學生累積練習經驗、增強自信心、自然學會使用日常英語溝通，並奠定日後英語學習的熱忱。

教學指引

先用 Warm Up 開場，以圖片配對詞彙的方式，幫助學生記住基礎詞彙。

Warm Up

A 根據圖片，從下方左右兩欄的選項中，各選出最符合的敘述，連接成完整的句子。

1 / 2 / 3 / 4 / 5 /

Ⓐ I cut myself
Ⓑ I fell over
Ⓒ I slipped
Ⓓ I got hit by a scooter
Ⓔ I fell off my bike

ⓐ while I was cycling by the river
ⓑ while I was chopping vegetables
ⓒ while I was walking my dog
ⓓ while I was running for the bus
ⓔ while I was crossing the road

B Pair Work 兩人一組，使用上方的連接完成的完整句練習對話。

Oh! Are you OK? — No, I had an accident.
What happened? — I cut myself while I was chopping vegetables.

46

接下來進入 Speak & Listen，先引導學生根據已提供的資訊與句型模板，將資訊代入練習口說，加強學生對關鍵資訊與句型的掌握力。

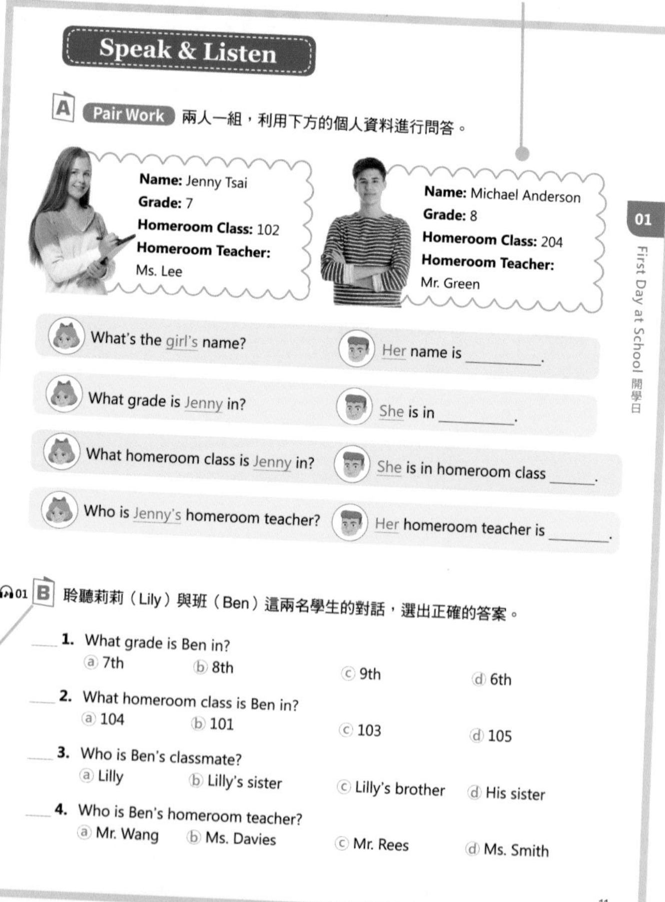

Speak & Listen

A Pair Work 兩人一組，利用下方的個人資料進行問答。

Name: Jenny Tsai
Grade: 7
Homeroom Class: 102
Homeroom Teacher: Ms. Lee

Name: Michael Anderson
Grade: 8
Homeroom Class: 204
Homeroom Teacher: Mr. Green

What's the girl's name? — Her name is ______.
What grade is Jenny in? — She is in ______.
What homeroom class is Jenny in? — She is in homeroom class ______.
Who is Jenny's homeroom teacher? — Her homeroom teacher is ______.

01 B 聆聽莉莉（Lily）與班（Ben）這兩名學生的對話，選出正確的答案。

___ 1. What grade is Ben in?
ⓐ 7th ⓑ 8th ⓒ 9th ⓓ 6th

___ 2. What homeroom class is Ben in?
ⓐ 104 ⓑ 101 ⓒ 103 ⓓ 105

___ 3. Who is Ben's classmate?
ⓐ Lilly ⓑ Lilly's sister ⓒ Lilly's brother ⓓ His sister

___ 4. Who is Ben's homeroom teacher?
ⓐ Mr. Wang ⓑ Ms. Davies ⓒ Mr. Rees ⓓ Ms. Smith

01 First Day at School 開學日

11

接著進行簡單的句型問答，讓學生套入詞彙並練習口說，先大致明白單字與句型的使用。

再以簡短對話的聽力練習，刺激學生抓出對話中的重要內容。

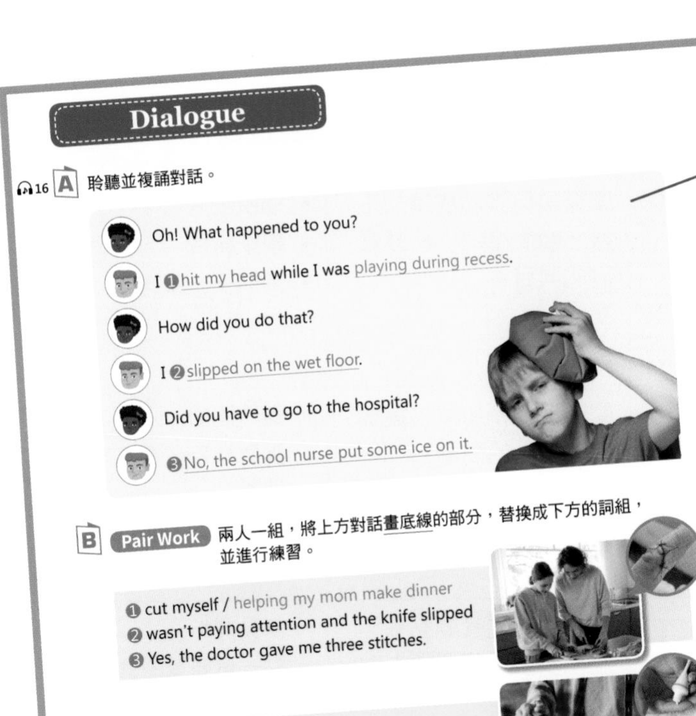

Dialogue

16 A 聆聽並複誦對話。

Oh! What happened to you?

I ❶hit my head while I was playing during recess.

How did you do that?

I ❷slipped on the wet floor.

Did you have to go to the hospital?

❸No, the school nurse put some ice on it.

B Pair Work 兩人一組，將上方對話畫底線的部分，替換成下方的詞組，並進行練習。

❶ cut myself / helping my mom make dinner
❷ wasn't paying attention and the knife slipped
❸ Yes, the doctor gave me three stitches.

❶ burned myself / making tea
❷ touched the hot kettle
❸ No, my mom put some ointment on it.

❶ broke my finger / playing soccer
❷ I tripped over my shoelaces
❸ Yes, they gave me an X-ray and then put my finger in plaster.

48

在Dialogue大題，讓學生先聆聽一段對話，注意對話重點的發音、語氣等，並進行複誦。

接著請學生將三組替換語句代入對話中，練習口語對話，透過模仿、重複與互動，加強對句型的印象。

最後的 Communicate 大題需要學生綜合單元所學，根據與單元相關的開放式問題，如要穿什麼衣服、要點什麼開胃菜、放學後的行程是什麼等，練習使用詞彙與句型自由作答，並和搭檔練習對話。

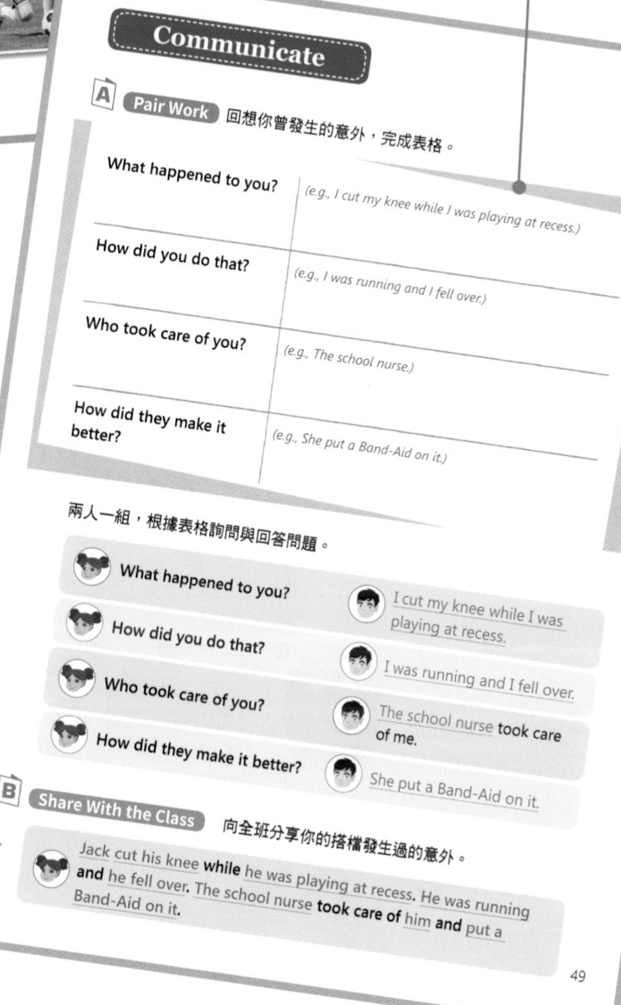

Communicate

A Pair Work 回想你曾發生的意外，完成表格。

What happened to you?	(e.g., I cut my knee while I was playing at recess.)
How did you do that?	(e.g., I was running and I fell over.)
Who took care of you?	(e.g., The school nurse.)
How did they make it better?	(e.g., She put a Band-Aid on it.)

兩人一組，根據表格詢問與回答問題。

What happened to you? — I cut my knee while I was playing at recess.

How did you do that? — I was running and I fell over.

Who took care of you? — The school nurse took care of me.

How did they make it better? — She put a Band-Aid on it.

B Share With the Class 向全班分享你的搭檔發生過的意外。

Jack cut his knee while he was playing at recess. He was running and he fell over. The school nurse took care of him and put a Band-Aid on it.

08 An Accident! 意外！

49

接著向全班分享自己或搭檔的回答，學會清晰地傳達與轉述資訊。

Contents Map

	聽說能力訓練	對話	溝通能力訓練
	• 詢問和回答某人的成績、班級和老師	• 談論班級和老師	• 談論你的課表 • 分享最喜歡的科目
	• 詢問和回答報名參加運動會活動的問題 • 說明為什麼你擅長某項運動	• 談論有參加哪些運動會活動以及競爭對手	• 猜測同學擅長哪一項運動 • 分享擅長的運動以及原因 • 運動的動詞
	• 配料 • 選擇喜歡的披薩／漢堡配料 • 幫客人點一份完整的餐點	• 用餐廳菜單點餐 • 詢問和回答想要的飲料種類	• 點夢幻餐點 • 與班上分享同學的夢幻餐點 • 更多餐點
	• 談論自己的休閒活動（喜歡做什麼、和誰一起做，以及多久做一次）	• 詢問某人的休閒活動 • 邀請某人加入你的活動	• 分組休閒活動賓果
	• 根據地圖問路和指路 • 估計步行到某處需要多長時間	• 詢問和指引詳細的方向，並估計到達目的地需要多久	• 根據同學的指示在地圖上識別位置 • 更多地點
	• 詢問和回答有關某人假期的問題，包括和誰一起去、做了什麼，以及是否享受這個假期	• 詢問某人的假期生活，以及他們是否參加了特定的活動	• 與同學分享你的假期故事 • 將同學的假期故事分享給班上
	• 詢問和回答有關想要寵物或有養寵物的問題，以及如何照顧牠們	• 談論飼養寵物的話題、描述寵物，並解釋如何照顧牠	• 提供關於自己飼養或想要的寵物資訊 • 猜測同學飼養／想要的寵物種類
	• 常見傷害 • 詢問和回答有關傷害及其發生的原因	• 談論最近一次發生的意外、如何發生的，以及怎麼處理這個意外	• 與同學分享一個意外故事 • 將同學的意外故事分享給班上

課程		目標	暖身活動
P. 50 **9** What Do You Want to Be? 你的志向是什麼？		學習談論未來想要做的工作、為什麼選擇這個職業，以及為了能夠做好這份工作可能需要的技能。	• 各種職業 • 想從事某項工作的原因 • 詢問某人長大後想成為什麼，以及原因
P. 54 **10** What's the Weather Like in Your Country? 你國家的天氣怎麼樣？		學習描述不同季節的天氣，根據天氣建議他人何時造訪不同的國家，並提出合適的穿著建議。	• 描述季節 • 各種天氣形容 • 詢問不同季節的天氣
P. 58 **11** How Will We Get There? 我們要如何到達那裡？		學習計劃一趟旅行、決定最佳的交通方式，並安排何時何地見面。	• 有趣的目的地 • 交通工具 • 為週末出遊建議一種交通工具
P. 62 **12** Good Manners 有禮貌		學習與表現失禮的人交談、禮貌地回應藉口，並建議替代的行為。	• 不良與良好禮儀 • 應對表現失禮的人
P. 66 **13** A Surprise 驚喜	Surprise!	學習根據朋友的興趣討論要買什麼禮物，以及如何送出禮物。	• 常見禮物項目 • 送給朋友禮物
P. 70 **14** What's Cooking? 你在做什麼？		學習談論烹飪／烘焙簡單的餐點，描述口味／餡料，並評論味道如何。	• 簡單的餐點 • 烘焙食品 • 詢問某人在煮什麼
P. 74 **15** What Do You Do After School? 你放學後會做什麼？		學習談論課外活動，包括家務、休閒活動和其他責任。	• 常見課後活動／責任 • 描述自己的課後活動
P. 80 **16** Save the Planet 守護地球		學習討論幫助環境的不同方法，以及如何提出對環境不友善行為的替代方案。	• 環境友善／不友善的行為 • 告訴某人為什麼他們不該做對環境有害的事情，並建議一個替代方案

	聽說能力訓練	對話	溝通能力訓練
	• 詢問和回答有關某人未來的職業 • 談論做好不同工作所需的技能	• 談論未來計畫、技能、熱情和興趣，以及追求特定職業所面臨的挑戰	• 根據同學的技能、熱情和個性建議一份職業
	• 詢問和回答有關不同國家的季節	• 談論到某人的國家度假，並準備適合當時天氣的衣服	• 給打算在不同時間來自己國家的人一些建議
	• 決定最適合搭乘哪種交通工具 • 決定出發前何時何地見面	• 談論參觀一個有趣的地方、決定最佳的旅行方式，以及出發前何時何地見面	• 和同學計劃一個有趣的週末（包括如何到達目的地和在哪碰面） • 和班上分享你們的週末計畫
	• 應對表現失禮的人，並回應其藉口	• 應對表現失禮的人、建議替代行為，並回應藉口	• 與同學進行爭論的角色扮演 • 與班上分享你們談論的內容
	• 根據某人的興趣討論要買什麼禮物	• 根據朋友喜歡和不喜歡的東西談論要為他們買什麼生日禮物	• 討論要為另一位同學買什麼禮物，並送給他們禮物
	• 不同口味／餡料 • 詢問和回答在烹飪什麼樣的菜，以及需要多長時間才能準備好 • 評論菜的味道	• 談論正在烹飪的菜，使用的口味／餡料是什麼，以及什麼時候能準備好 • 詢問和回答一道菜的味道如何	• 為朋友規劃一道菜 • 角色扮演試吃朋友的菜並評論味道
	• 詢問和回答某人的課後活動	• 提供詳細的課後活動行程	• 與同學分享你的課後活動 • 與班上分享你和同學課後活動的相似與相異之處
	• 討論對環境不友善行為的替代方案 • 說服某人改變他們的行為	• 根據所在的地方，談論拯救地球的不同方式	• 討論在學校期間可以做些什麼來拯救環境 • 以班級決定採取一些環保行動措施

Contents

Unit 01

First Day at School 開學日

Warm Up

將圖片與詞彙配對。

1 

2 

3 

4 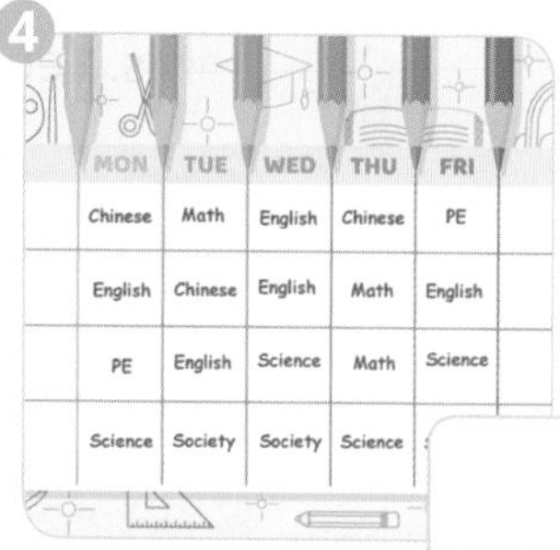

5 

6 

7 

8 

9 

10 

11 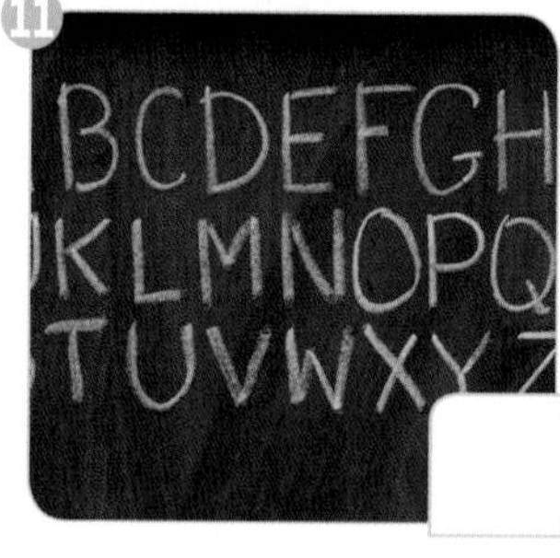

12 

ⓐ Chinese	ⓑ science	ⓒ history	ⓓ math
ⓔ homeroom class	ⓕ grade	ⓖ music	ⓗ English
ⓘ homeroom teacher	ⓙ art	ⓚ class schedule	ⓛ geography

Pair Work 兩人一組，使用上方的學科練習對話。

 What's our next class today?

 Our next class is math.

Speak & Listen

A Pair Work 兩人一組，利用下方的個人資料進行問答。

Name: Jenny Tsai
Grade: 7
Homeroom Class: 102
Homeroom Teacher: Ms. Lee

Name: Michael Anderson
Grade: 8
Homeroom Class: 204
Homeroom Teacher: Mr. Green

 What's the girl's name?

 Her name is ________.

 What grade is Jenny in?

 She is in ________.

 What homeroom class is Jenny in?

 She is in homeroom class ______.

 Who is Jenny's homeroom teacher?

 Her homeroom teacher is ______.

01 B 聆聽莉莉（Lily）與班（Ben）這兩名學生的對話，選出正確的答案。

____ **1.** What grade is Ben in?
ⓐ 7th ⓑ 8th ⓒ 9th ⓓ 6th

____ **2.** What homeroom class is Ben in?
ⓐ 104 ⓑ 101 ⓒ 103 ⓓ 105

____ **3.** Who is Ben's classmate?
ⓐ Lilly ⓑ Lilly's sister ⓒ Lilly's brother ⓓ His sister

____ **4.** Who is Ben's homeroom teacher?
ⓐ Mr. Wang ⓑ Ms. Davies ⓒ Mr. Rees ⓓ Ms. Smith

Dialogue

02 A 聆聽並複誦對話。

Hi! Are you in grade 7, too?

Yes, I am. What homeroom class are you in?

I'm in class ❶ 103. And you?

I'm in 102. Are there many students in your class?

Yes, there are ❷ thirty-five.

Who is your homeroom teacher?

My homeroom teacher is ❸ Mr. Yang. Oh! It's time for my next class! Talk to you later!

Pair Work 兩人一組，將上方對話畫底線的部分，替換成下方的詞組，並進行練習。

❶ 104
❷ thirty-four
❸ Ms. Jones

❶ 105
❷ thirty-two
❸ Mr. Smith

❶ 101
❷ thirty-one
❸ Ms. Huang

Communicate

Pair Work 兩人一組，看看下方的課表，輪流詢問對方的課表。

	Monday	Tuesday	Wednesday	Thursday	Friday
1st Period	Chinese	History	English	Math	Chinese
2nd Period	Math	Chinese	History	English	History
3rd Period	Math	English	Geography	Science	English
4th Period	Science	English	Science	Geography	Science
5th Period	English	Science	Chinese	Music	Science
6th Period	Geography	Art	Chinese	Art	Music
7th Period	Music	Math	Music	Chinese	Math

What do we have for 2nd period on Thursday?

We have English.

Share With the Class 看看自己的課表，向全班分享你最喜歡的科目與上課的時間。

My favorite subject is English.
I have English for 3rd period on Monday.

Unit 02

Sports Day 運動會

Warm Up

詹姆斯與安妮做不同的運動。根據圖片，判斷下方句子是誰說的，詹姆斯（James）寫 J，安妮（Annie）寫 A。

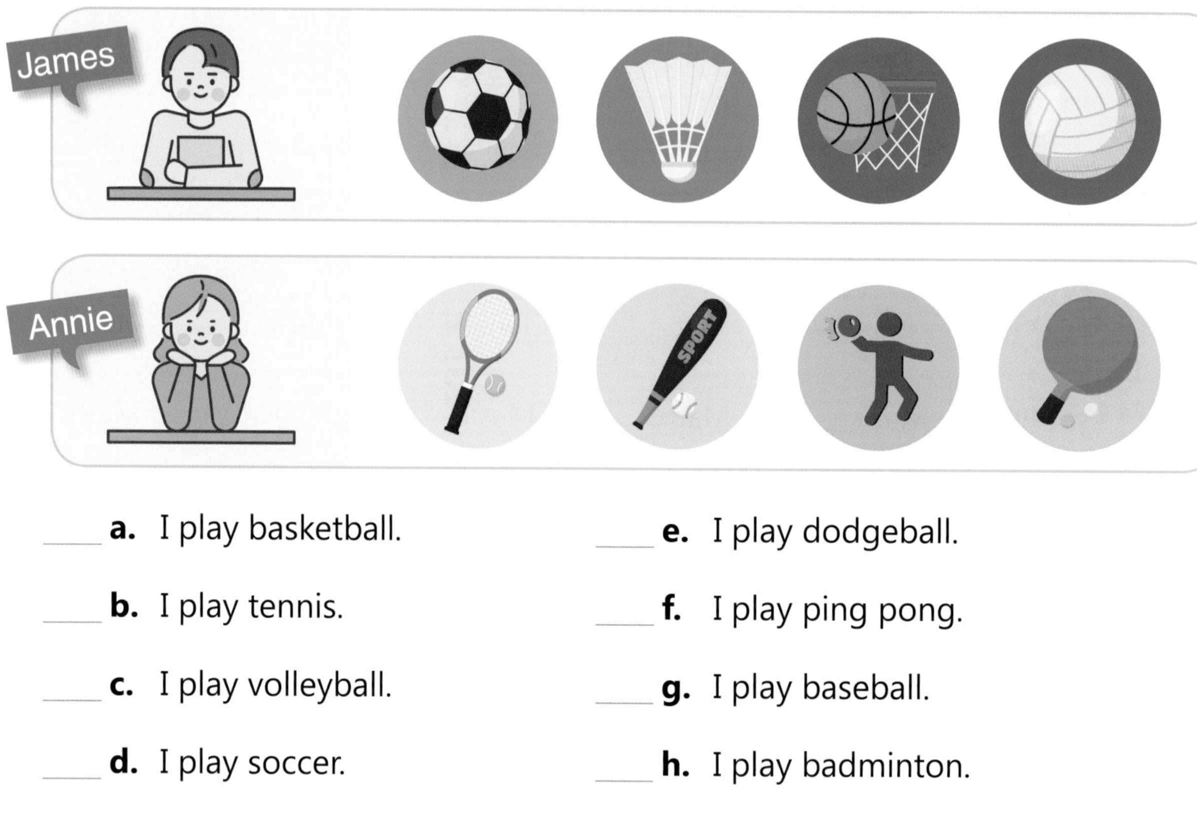

____ **a.** I play basketball.

____ **b.** I play tennis.

____ **c.** I play volleyball.

____ **d.** I play soccer.

____ **e.** I play dodgeball.

____ **f.** I play ping pong.

____ **g.** I play baseball.

____ **h.** I play badminton.

Pair Work 兩人一組，使用上方的運動項目練習對話。

 Does James play basketball?

 Yes, he does.

 Do you play basketball?

 No, I don't.

Speak & Listen

Pair Work 下禮拜就是學校的運動會了！在你想報名參加的運動項目旁打 ✓。

basketball game

running race

badminton tournament

long jump

兩人一組，配對上方的運動項目與下方的動作，並練習對話。

jumping far	shooting the ball into the basket
hitting the ball over the net	running fast

What do you want to sign up for?

I want to sign up for the basketball game.

Why do you want to sign up for the basketball game?

Because I'm pretty good at shooting the ball into the basket.

03 B 聆聽凱特（Kate）與李奇（Rich）這兩名學生的對話，並完成表格。

Who				
Event	badminton tournament			ping pong tournament
Start Time		9:00	10:00	

Dialogue

04 A 明天就是學校的運動會了！聆聽並複誦對話。

Are you enjoying sports day so far?

Yes, I'm having a great time.

Do you have any events later?

Yes, I have a ❶ volleyball game later.

At what time?

❷ Two o'clock.

Who are you competing against?

❸ We're playing against class 106.

Good luck!

Pair Work 兩人一組，將上方對話畫底線的部分，替換成下方的詞組，並進行練習。

❶ dodgeball game
❷ Eleven thirty
❸ We are playing against class 101

❶ badminton tournament
❷ Nine o'clock
❸ My first game is against Kay Green from class 203

❶ running race
❷ One forty-five
❸ I'm running against John, Jim, Mike, and Steve

Communicate

A **Pair Work** 你擅長什麼運動？填寫下方的圖表。

Sport: ______________________

Do you play as part of a team?	Yes / No
Do you use a ball?	Yes / No
Do you use a racket or a bat?	Yes / No

兩人一組，詢問下方的問題，猜出對方擅長的運動。

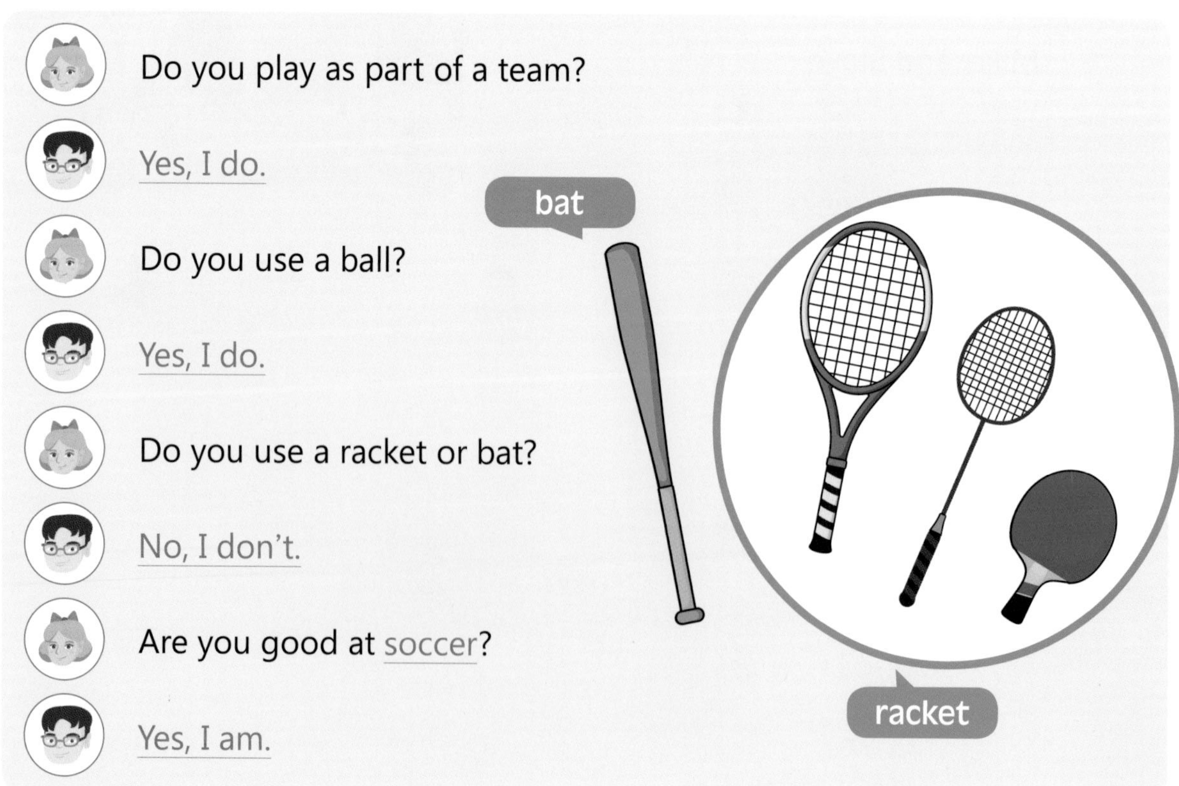

Do you play as part of a team?

Yes, I do.

Do you use a ball?

Yes, I do.

Do you use a racket or bat?

No, I don't.

Are you good at soccer?

Yes, I am.

Share With the Class

向全班分享為何你擅長某項運動，可以使用下方的詞彙練習。

The sport I'm good at is soccer. I'm good at it because I can catch very well.

... very well

basketball / shoot

football / tackle

basketball / block

basketball / pass

soccer / catch

... very fast

ping pong / serve

hockey / move

running / run

... very hard

baseball / hit

baseball / throw

Unit 03

At a Restaurant 在餐廳

Warm Up

 看看下方的菜單，使用下頁的 Word Box 字彙，填入菜單的空格中。

Dino's American Restaurant

Appetizers

Caesar ______

Tomato ______

______ Wings

Main Courses

______

______ and ______

______

______

______

Chocolate ______

Apple ______

______

______

Iced ______

Orange ______

Word Box

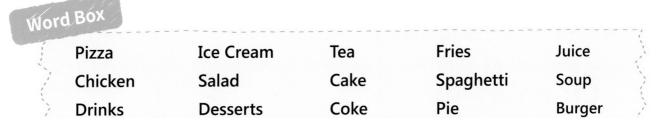

Pizza	Ice Cream	Tea	Fries	Juice
Chicken	Salad	Cake	Spaghetti	Soup
Drinks	Desserts	Coke	Pie	Burger

B **Pair Work** 兩人一組，使用上頁菜單裡的菜餚與飲品，練習對話。

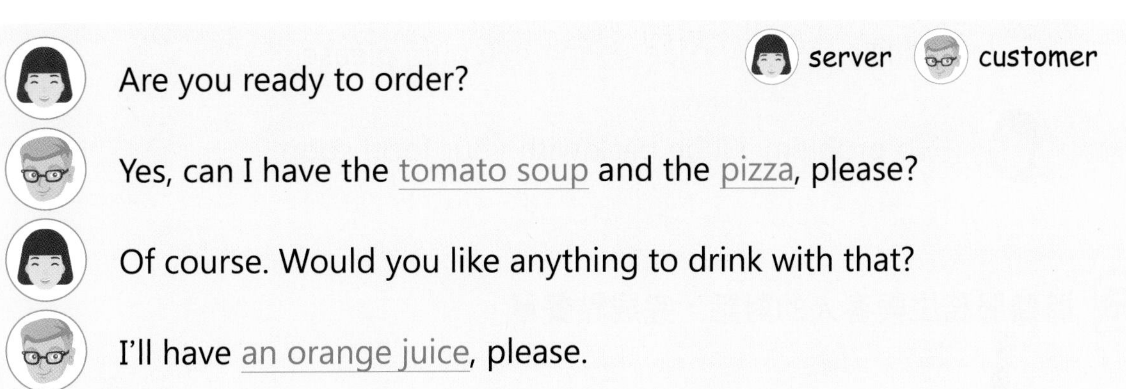

server
customer
Are you ready to order?
Yes, can I have the tomato soup and the pizza, please?
Of course. Would you like anything to drink with that?
I'll have an orange juice, please.

Speak & Listen

A **Pair Work** 你想點披薩還是漢堡？選出一個，再圈出你想要加的配料。

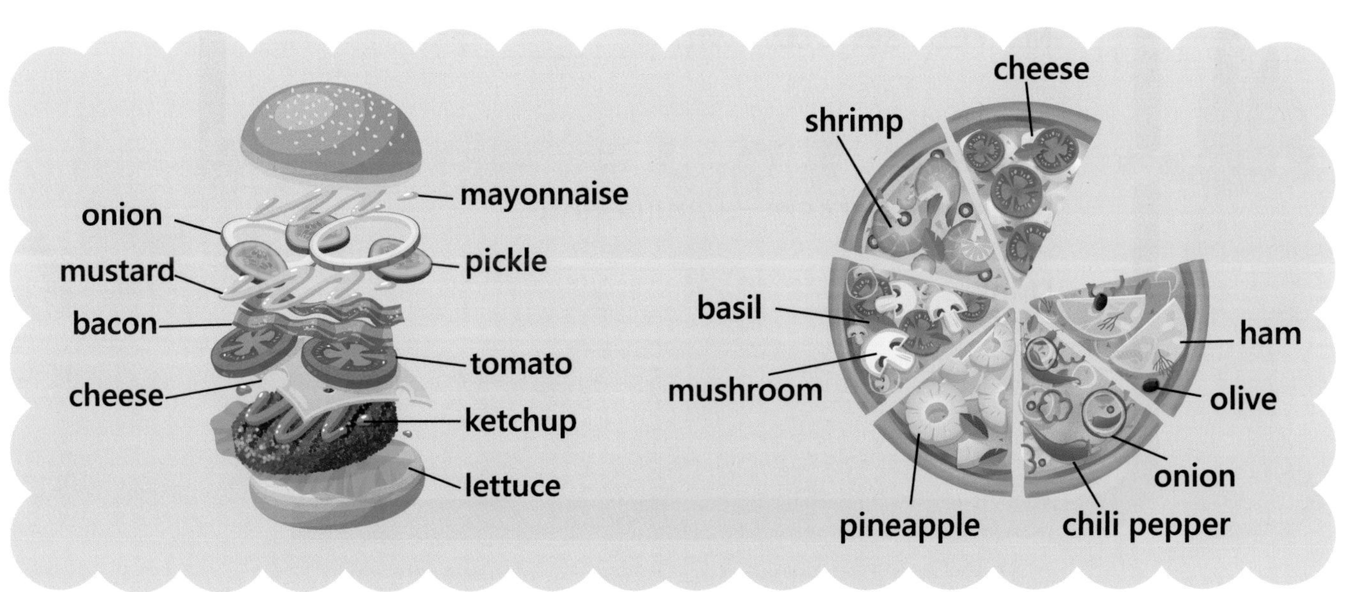

兩人一組，運用上頁的回答練習對話。

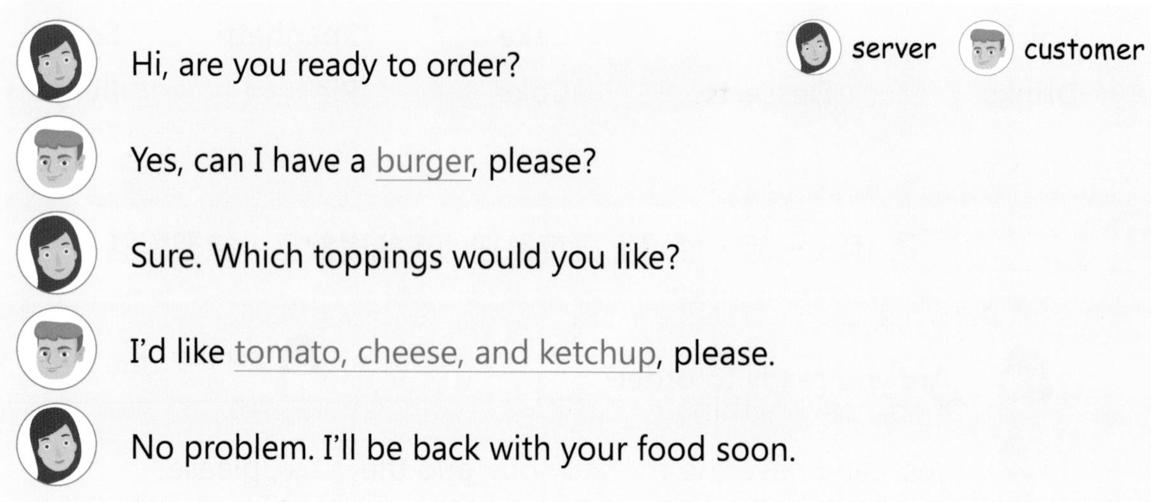

server
customer
Hi, are you ready to order?
Yes, can I have a burger, please?
Sure. Which toppings would you like?
I'd like tomato, cheese, and ketchup, please.
No problem. I'll be back with your food soon.

05 **B** 聆聽服務生與客人的對話，完成點餐單。

Order Form

Table: *5*

Appetizers: ____________

Main Courses: *pizza with* ________, *onion, and* ________

Dessert: *ice cream—vanilla and* ________

Drinks: ________

Dialogue

06 A 你正在餐廳裡點晚餐。聆聽並複誦對話。

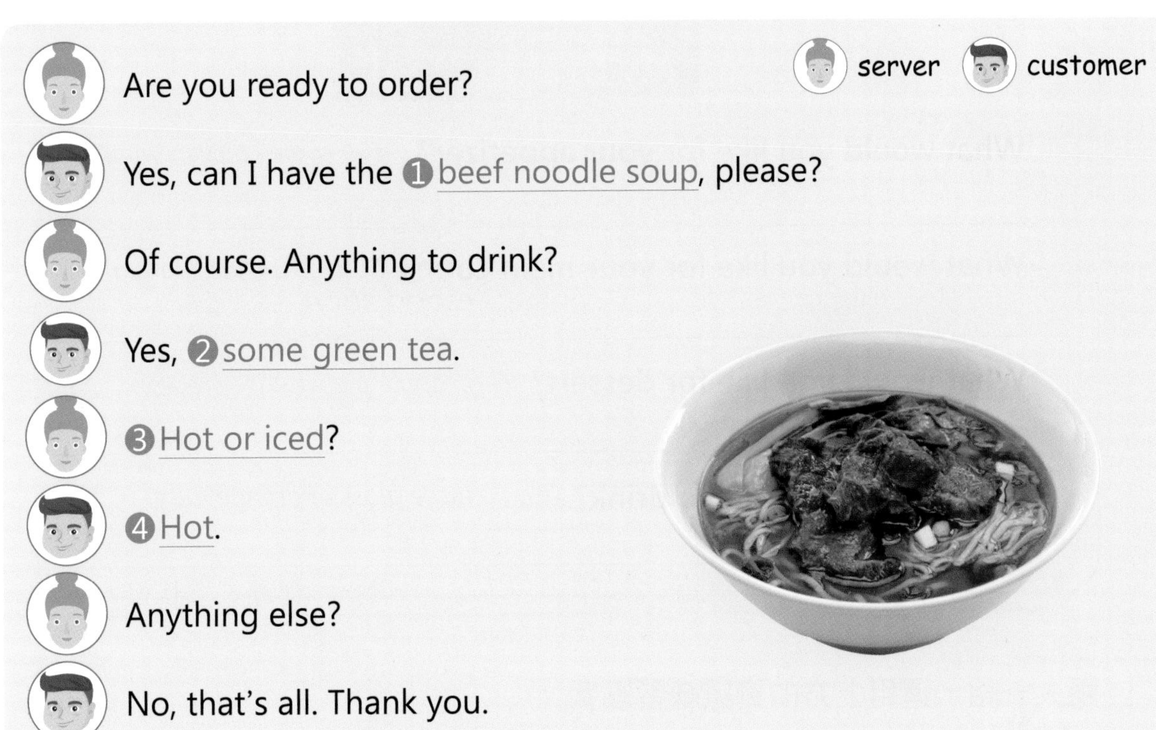

server / customer

Are you ready to order?

Yes, can I have the ❶ beef noodle soup, please?

Of course. Anything to drink?

Yes, ❷ some green tea.

❸ Hot or iced?

❹ Hot.

Anything else?

No, that's all. Thank you.

B **Pair Work** 兩人一組，將上方對話畫底線的部分，替換成下方的詞組，並進行練習。

❶ chicken burger
❷ a glass of Coke
❸ small, medium, or large
❹ [you choose]

❶ steak and potatoes
❷ a glass of water
❸ still or sparkling
❹ [you choose]

❶ blueberry pancakes
❷ a cup of coffee
❸ with milk or without milk
❹ [you choose]

Communicate

Pair Work 你的夢幻餐點是什麼？回答下方的問題。可以使用下頁的補充字彙。

My Dream Meal

What would you like for your appetizer? *(e.g., some chicken wings)*

____

What would you like for your main course? *(e.g., a cheese pizza)*

____

What would you like for dessert? *(e.g., apple pie with ice cream)*

____

What would you like to drink? *(e.g., a large glass of orange juice)*

____

兩人一組，運用上方的資訊練習點餐。

server / customer

Server: Hi, are you ready to order?

Customer: Yes, can I have ______________ to start?

Server: No problem. And for your main course?

Customer: For my main course I'd like ______________.

Server: OK, and for dessert?

Customer: For dessert, I'd like ______________.

Server: Anything to drink?

Customer: Yes, ______________, please.

Share With the Class 向全班分享你搭檔的夢幻餐點。

For his dream meal, Ben would like ice cream for an appetizer, steak for his main course, cheese cake for dessert, and juice to drink.

Extra Vocabulary

onion ring 洋蔥圈

cheese stick 起司條

garlic bread 大蒜麵包

oyster 牡蠣

omelet 歐姆蛋

lasagne 千層麵

fried rice 炒飯

curry rice 咖哩飯

waffle 鬆餅

pudding 布丁

milkshake 奶昔

Americano 美式咖啡

Unit 04

What Do You Like to Do in Your Free Time? 你空閒時喜歡做什麼？

Warm Up

A 根據圖片，將形容動作的詞彙，與正確圖片配對。

James

Charlie

May

Lisa

Fred

Joe

Nick

Sue

ⓐ play guitar ⓑ do puzzles ⓒ bake ⓓ do kung fu
ⓔ read ⓕ play chess ⓖ go hiking ⓗ play online games

B **Pair Work** 兩人一組，使用上方的動作詞彙練習對話。

What do you like to do in your free time, James?

I like to play chess. What do you like to do in your free time, Sue?

I like to read.

Speak & Listen

Pair Work 你在空閒時間喜歡做什麼？你有多常做這件事？想想看，填入表格。

What? ________________

How often?

☑ Mon. ☑ Tue. ☑ Wed. ☑ Thur. ☑ Fri. ☑ Sat. ☑ Sun.	☑ Mon. ☐ Tue. ☐ Wed. ☐ Thur. ☐ Fri. ☐ Sat. ☐ Sun.	☑ Mon. ☑ Tue. ☐ Wed. ☐ Thur. ☐ Fri. ☐ Sat. ☐ Sun.
every day	once a week	twice a week
☑ Mon. ☑ Tue. ☐ Wed. ☑ Thur. ☐ Fri. ☐ Sat. ☐ Sun.	☑ Mon. ☑ Tue. ☐ Wed. ☑ Thur. ☑ Fri. ☐ Sat. ☑ Sun.	☐ Mon. ☐ Tue. ☐ Wed. ☐ Thur. ☐ Fri. ☑ Sat. ☑ Sun.
three times a week	most days	on weekends

With who?

by myself	with my mom/dad/ family	with my friends
with a class	with a coach	with a group/club

兩人一組，運用上方的內容練習對話。

 What do like to do in your free time?

 I like to go hiking.

 Nice! How often do you go hiking?

 I go hiking on weekends.

 Who do you do it with?

 I do it with my family.

07 **B** 聆聽雷（Ray）與貝拉（Bella）的對話，並完成表格。

Who?	Ray	Bella
What?		
How often?		
With whom?		

Dialogue

08 **A** 聆聽並複誦對話。

What do you like to do in your free time?

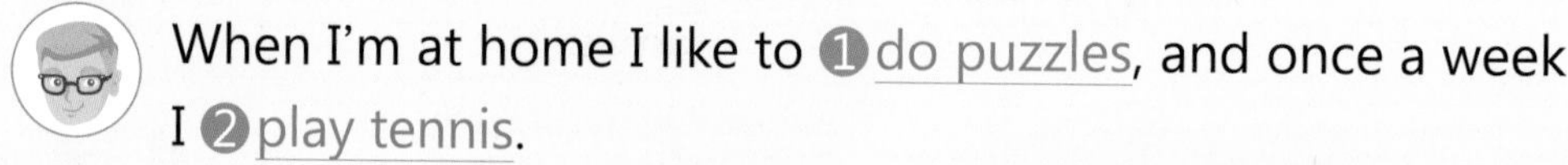

When I'm at home I like to ❶ do puzzles, and once a week I ❷ play tennis.

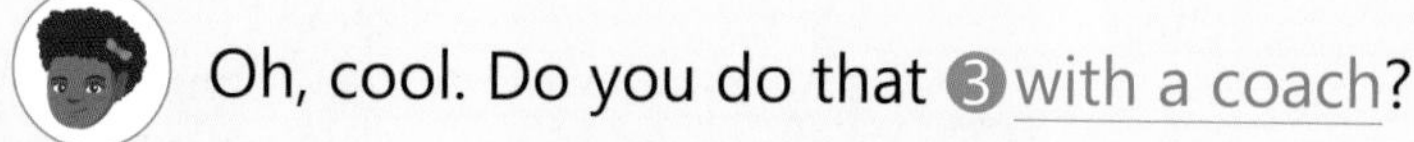

Oh, cool. Do you do that ❸ with a coach?

No, I do it ❹ with my friends.

That sounds fun.

Maybe you can join us sometime!

Thanks! I'd love to!

 **Pair Work** 兩人一組，將上頁對話畫底線的部分，替換成下方的詞組，並進行練習。

1. play guitar
2. do yoga
3. by yourself
4. with a class

1. play online games
2. go fishing
3. with a club
4. with my dad

1. paint
2. go hiking
3. with your family
4. with a hiking group

Communicate

Class Work 在三個項目下各填入三個例子，完成賓果卡。

BINGO!		
Activity (e.g., go swimming)	How often? (e.g., every day)	With who? (e.g., my mom)

現在來玩賓果遊戲！在教室內四處走動，詢問同學下方的問題，並用賓果卡的內容來回答。

What do you like to do in your free time?
I like to go swimming in my free time.

How often do you go swimming? I go swimming every day.

Who do you go swimming with? I go swimming with my mom.

遇到有人的答案與你的相同，就在那一格打叉；當三個叉連成一條線時就贏了，此時要大喊「Bingo」！

Unit 05

Asking for Directions 問路

Warm Up

A 地圖裡的各是什麼地點？將圖片與字彙配對。

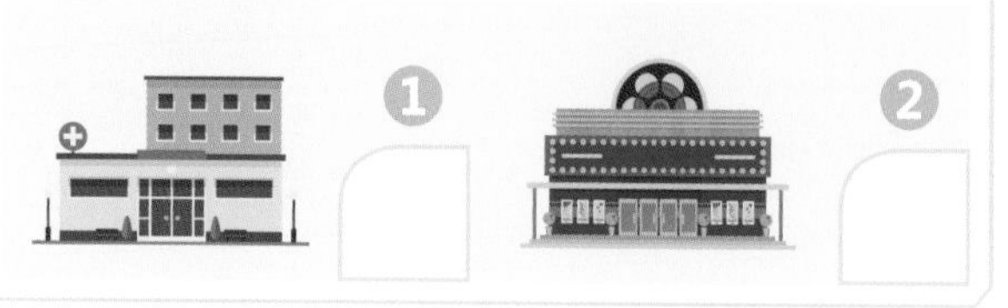

Third Street

Fourth Street

Main Street

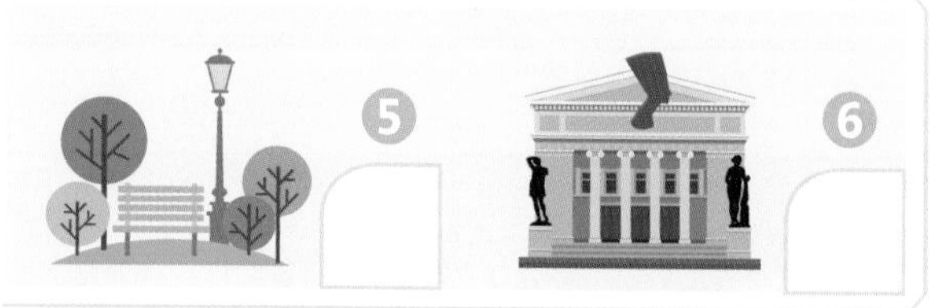

First Street

Second Street

ⓐ restaurant	ⓑ hospital	ⓒ park	ⓓ bookstore
ⓔ museum	ⓕ movie theater	ⓖ café	ⓗ bakery
ⓘ supermarket	ⓙ school	ⓚ bank	ⓛ post office

B **Pair Work** 兩人一組，使用上方的地圖練習對話。

Hi, is there a restaurant near here?

Yes, there's one on Second Street. It's next to the supermarket.

Thank you!

Speak & Listen

 **Pair Work** 兩人一組，先從地圖上選出你想去的地方，再向你的搭檔問路。

Fifth Street

Sixth Street

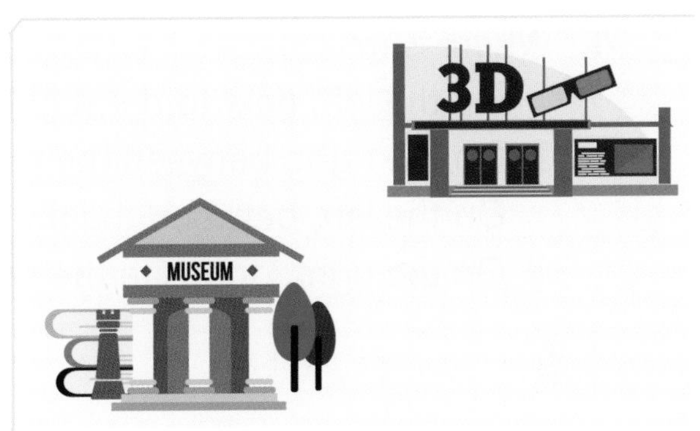

Main Street

Third Street

Fourth Street

First Street

Second Street

You're here!

 Excuse me. Is there a post office near here?

 Yes. Go straight for two blocks. Turn right onto Fourth Street. The post office is on your right.

09 **B** 麥克斯（Max）是鎮上新來的。聆聽他向陌生人問話的對話，選出正確的答案。

____ **1.** What is Max looking for?
ⓐ A museum. ⓑ A cafe. ⓒ A bookstore. ⓓ A supermarket.

____ **2.** What street is it on?
ⓐ First Street. ⓑ Main Street. ⓒ Fifth Street. ⓓ Third Street.

____ **3.** How long will it take to walk there?
ⓐ Five minutes. ⓑ Ten minutes. ⓒ Two minutes. ⓓ Fifteen minutes.

____ **4.** Where is it?
ⓐ On the left, next to the school.
ⓑ On the right, between the café and the museum.
ⓒ On the left, between the museum and the park.
ⓓ On the right, opposite the museum.

Dialogue

 A 聆聽並複誦對話。

 Excuse me. Could you help me? I'm looking for ❶ the City Zoo.

 Yes, I know it. It's on ❷ Second Street.

 Is that far? Should I take a taxi?

 No, it only takes around ❸ fifteen minutes on foot.

 OK. How do I get there from here?

 Go straight for ❹ three blocks. Turn right. And it's on your left, next to the museum.

 Great. Thank you so much for your help!

 **Pair Work** 兩人一組，將上方對話畫底線的部分，替換成下方的詞組，並進行練習。

❶ Tony's Italian Restaurant ❷ Main Street ❸ five
❹ two / left / right / opposite the post office

❶ the Modern Art Museum ❷ Seventh Street
❸ fifteen
❹ four / left / left / between the bank and the bookstore

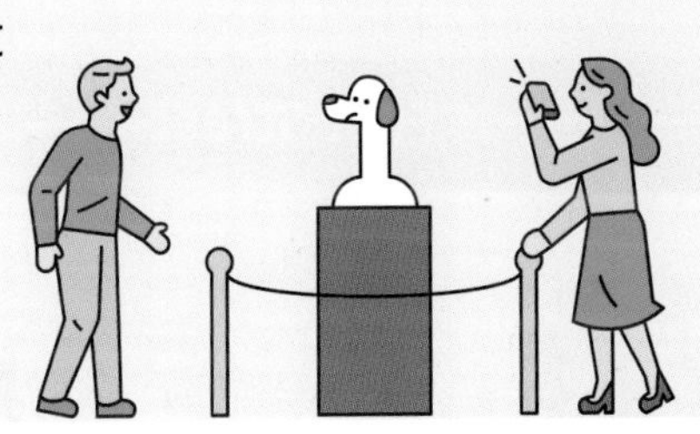

❶ the Golden Mall ❷ First Street ❸ two
❹ one / right / right / opposite the police station

Communicate

Pair Work 兩人一組，先根據指示完成你那部分的地圖。

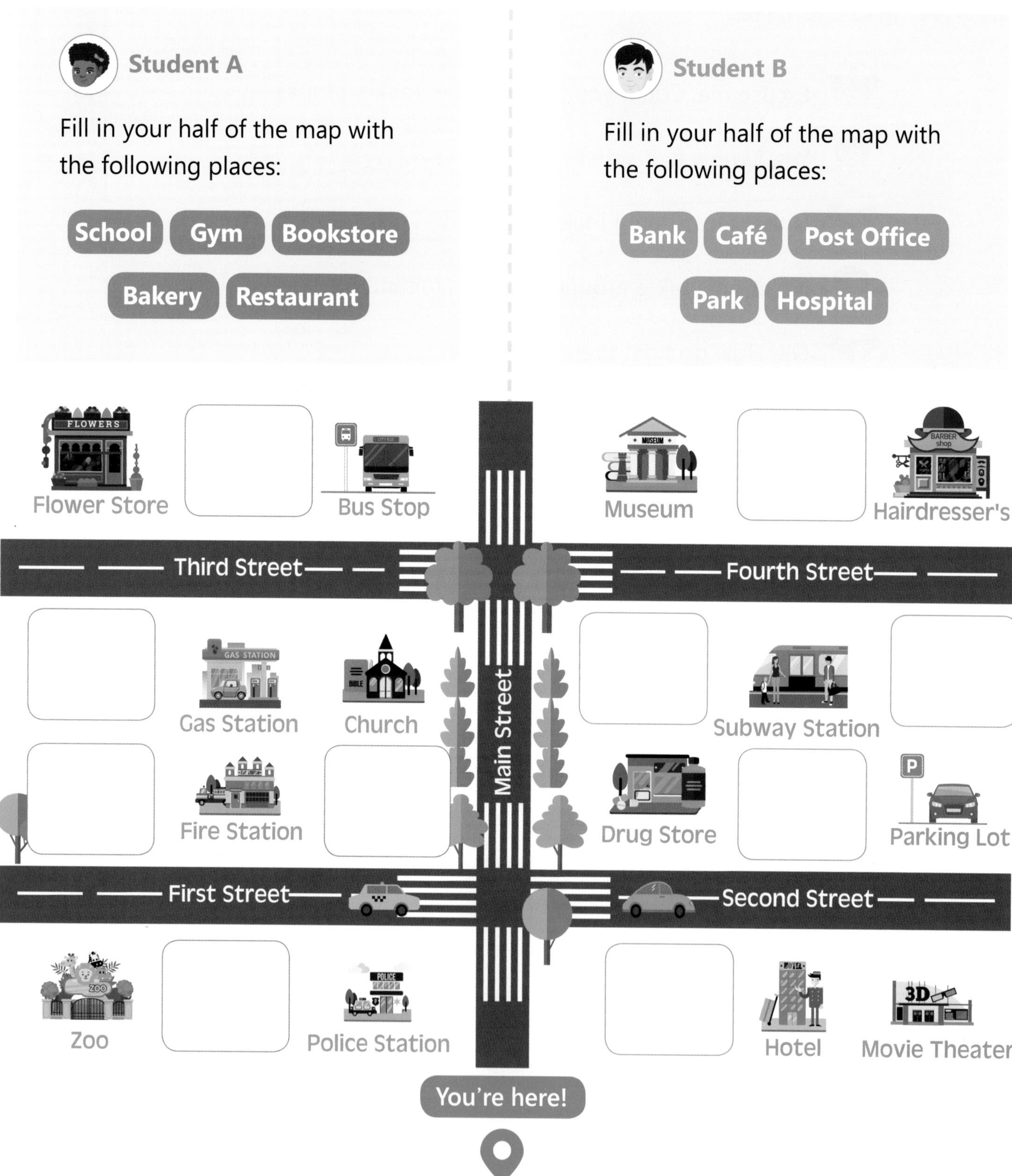

Student A
Fill in your half of the map with the following places:
School
Gym
Bookstore
Bakery
Restaurant
Student B
Fill in your half of the map with the following places:
Bank
Café
Post Office
Park
Hospital
FLOWERS
Flower Store
Bus Stop
MUSEUM
Museum
BARBER shop
Hairdresser's
Third Street
Fourth Street
GAS STATION
Gas Station
BIBLE
Church
Main Street
Subway Station
Fire Station
Drug Store
P
Parking Lot
First Street
Second Street
ZOO
Zoo
POLICE
Police Station
Hotel
3D
Movie Theater
You're here!

詢問搭檔下方的問題，根據他的回答，完成他那部分的地圖。

Excuse me, where's the nearest __________?

____________________________________.

完成後，請對照兩人的地圖，你們的答案是一樣的嗎？

Extra Vocabulary

library
圖書館

kindergarten
幼稚園

phone repair shop
手機維修店

temple
寺廟

airport
機場

gym
健身中心

convenience store
便利商店

department store
百貨公司

aquarium
水族館

planetarium
天文館

concert hall
音樂廳

botanical garden
植物園

Unit 06

Your Summer Vacation 你的暑假

Warm Up

A 將下框中的國家名及活動與圖片配對。

Ⓐ Thailand Ⓑ Japan Ⓒ Australia Ⓓ USA
Ⓔ Italy Ⓕ UK Ⓖ China Ⓗ France

Ⓘ I walked on the Great Wall.
Ⓙ I climbed Mount Fuji.
Ⓚ I visited Buckingham Palace.
Ⓛ I ate lots of delicious pizza.
Ⓜ I saw a kangaroo and a koala bear!
Ⓝ I played on the beach and swam in the sea.
Ⓞ I took a photo in front of the Eiffel Tower.
Ⓟ I went to the top of the Statue of Liberty.

 **Pair Work** 兩人一組，使用前頁的國家名與活動練習對話。

 Where did you go for your summer vacation this year?

 I went to Japan.

 Wow! Sounds great! What did you do there?

 I climbed Mount Fuji. It was so much fun!

Speak & Listen

 **Pair Work** 兩人一組，根據安妮（Anne）出遊時拍的照片進行問答。

 Where did Anne go for her summer vacation?

 She went to ________.

 Who did she go with?

 She went with her ________.

 What did she do?

 She ________, ________, and ________.

 Did she have fun?

 Yes, ________.

11 B 聆聽尼克（Nick）與碧（Bea）這兩名學生關於暑假的對話，並完成表格。

	Nick	Bea
Where?		
With whom?		
What did he/she do?		
Was it fun?		

Dialogue

 聆聽並複誦對話。

 Did you go anywhere fun for your summer vacation?

 Yes, I did. I went to ❶ the UK with my family.

 Oh, nice! I went there ❷ last year. Did you ❸ visit Buckingham Palace?

 Yes, we did, and we ❹ went biking in the countryside.

 It sounds like you had a great time!

 I did! I hope I can go there again someday.

Pair Work 兩人一組，將上方對話畫底線的部分，替換成下方的詞組，並進行練習。

1. Thailand
2. two years ago
3. eat a lot of phad thai
4. went shopping in the street markets

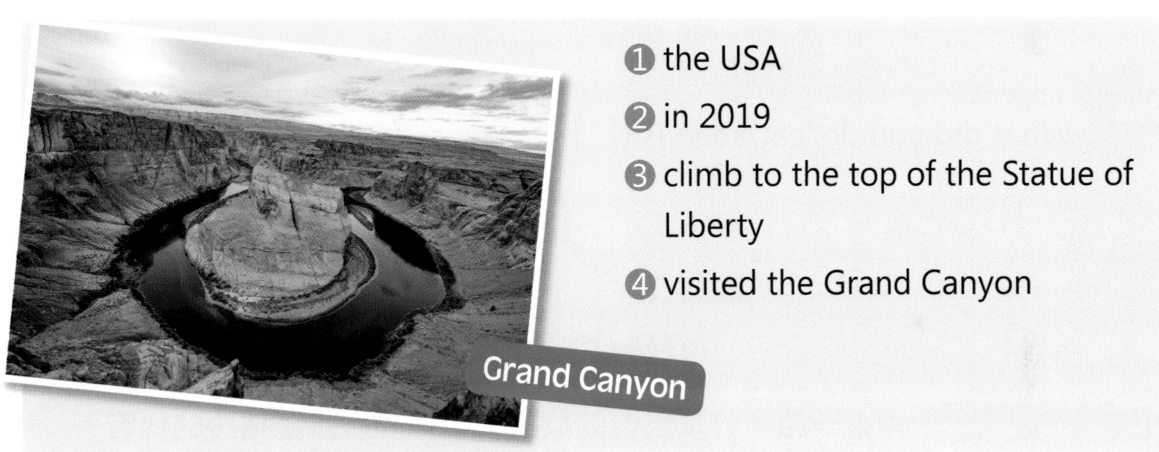

1. the USA
2. in 2019
3. climb to the top of the Statue of Liberty
4. visited the Grand Canyon

1. France
2. when I was twelve
3. take a photo in front of the Eiffel Tower
4. visited lots of famous art museums

Communicate

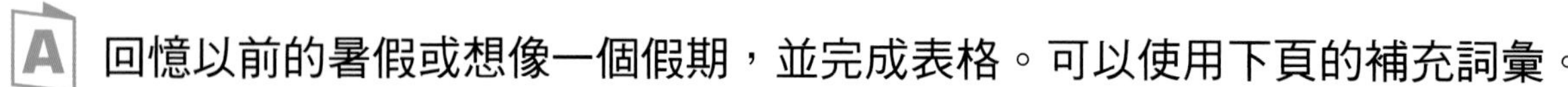

A 回憶以前的暑假或想像一個假期，並完成表格。可以使用下頁的補充詞彙。

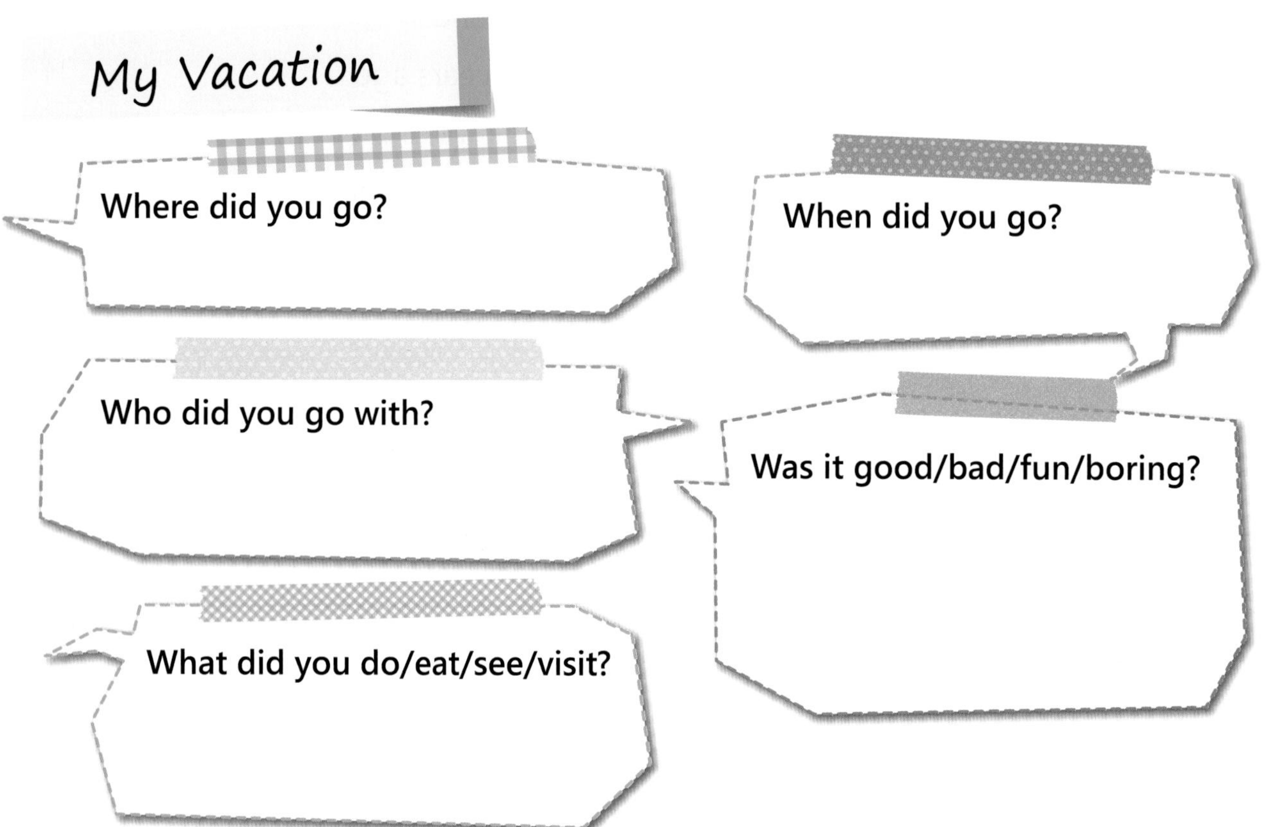

My Vacation
Where did you go?
When did you go?
Who did you go with?
Was it good/bad/fun/boring?
What did you do/eat/see/visit?

B **Pair Work** 兩人一組，分享出遊的故事，並仔細聆聽搭檔說的內容。

In the summer of 2019, I went to Australia with my grandparents. I went surfing and I saw a kangaroo and a koala bear. It was a really fun vacation.

Share With the Class 向全班分享搭檔的假期故事。

Example

In the summer of 2019, Joe went to Italy . . .

Extra Vocabulary

go skiing
滑雪

go camping
露營

go diving
潛水

go sailing
帆船航行

visit a castle
參訪城堡

visit a temple
參訪寺廟

buy a souvenir
買紀念品

take a tour
參加導覽

go to a festival
參加節慶

go on safari
觀察野生動物

go to a hot spring
泡溫泉

go to a concert
去演唱會

Unit 07

Do You Have a Pet?
你有養寵物嗎？

Warm Up

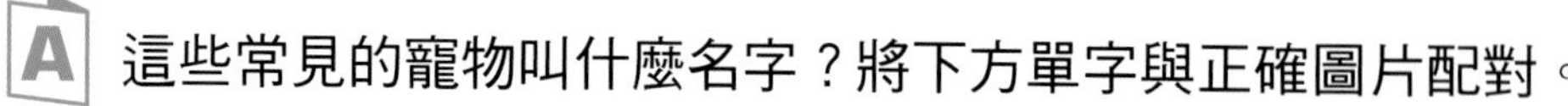

A 這些常見的寵物叫什麼名字？將下方單字與正確圖片配對。

1 
○○ ______________

2 
○○ ______________

3 
○○ ______________

4 
○○ ______________

5 
○○ ______________

6 
○○ ______________

7 
○○ ______________

8 
○○ ______________

snake	turtle	rabbit	tropical fish
parrot	dog/puppy	cat/kitten	mouse

從下方選出兩個形容詞來描述寵物，把字母寫在寵物名稱前的圓形框中。

ⓐ friendly	ⓑ cute	ⓒ playful	ⓓ quiet	ⓔ smart
ⓕ loving	ⓖ colorful	ⓗ soft	ⓘ funny	ⓙ interesting

B Pair Work 兩人一組，使用前頁的寵物名與形容詞對話。

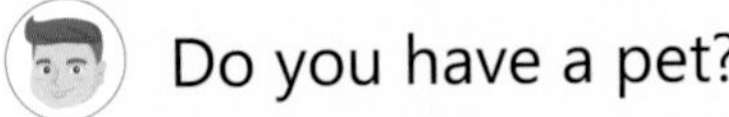
Do you have a pet?

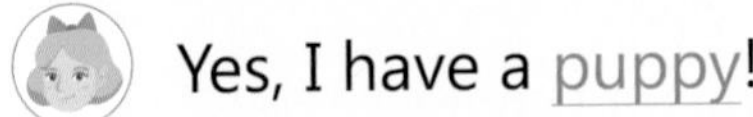
Yes, I have a puppy!

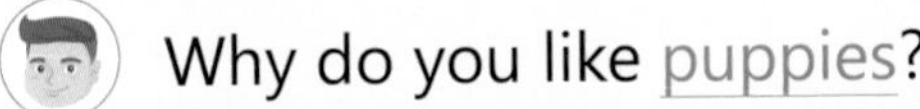
Why do you like puppies?

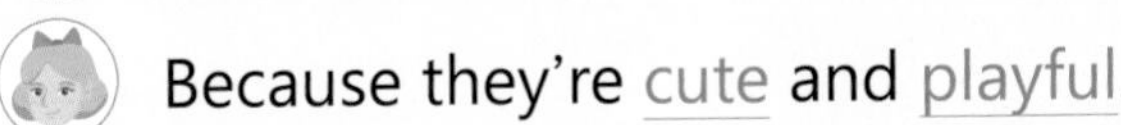
Because they're cute and playful.

Speak & Listen

A Pair Work 根據照顧寵物的方式，把正確的寵物名稱填入框內。

dog　cat　parrot　tropical fish

How do you take care of your pet?

[　　]	[　　]	[　　]	[　　]
1 Clean its litter box twice a week. 2 Play with it often. 3 Feed it twice a day.	1 Change its water once a week. 2 Feed it once a day. 3 Buy some plants for its bowl.	1 Clean its cage once a week. 2 Make sure it has enough food and water. 3 Talk to it often.	1 Take it for walks every day. 2 Feed it twice a day. 3 Play with it often.

兩人一組，根據上方表格內的資訊練習對話。

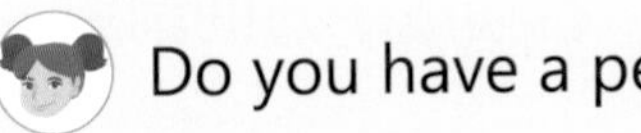
Do you have a pet?

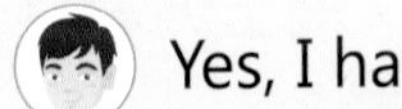
Yes, I have a parrot.

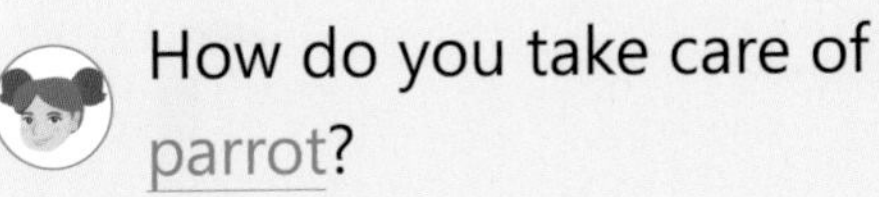
How do you take care of a parrot?

You have to clean its cage once a week, make sure it has enough food and water, and talk to it often.

That sounds like a lot of work.

It is, but it's worth it!

13 **B** 吉姆（Jim）想要飼養寵物。聆聽他與莎莉（Sally）的對話，再將下列句中錯誤的部分劃掉，改上正確的內容。

1. Jim wants to get a new kitten.

2. Sally says Jim should feed his new pet two times a day.

3. Sally says Jim should walk his new pet for a long walk once a day.

4. Jim thinks that taking care of this pet will be easy.

Dialogue

14 **A** 聆聽並複誦對話。

Do you have a pet at home?

Yes, I have a ❶ rabbit.

What are they like as pets?

They're ❷ playful and cute.

Are they hard to take care of?

Well, you have to ❸ feed them plenty of vegetables and brush their fur regularly.

That's not too bad. They sound like great pets!

Pair Work 兩人一組，將上方對話畫底線的部分，替換成下方的詞組，並進行練習。

❶ snake
❷ quiet / interesting
❸ clean their tank regularly / feed them once a week

1 mouse
2 soft / friendly
3 clean their cage regularly / give them lots of toys to play with

1 kitten
2 funny / playful
3 feed them often / give them lots of attention

Communicate

Pair Work 你有養寵物嗎？完成下方圖表。如果沒有養寵物，則可以根據想要養的寵物作答。

Your pet:

Describe it using at least 2 adjectives. *(e.g., shy, loud . . .)*	
Write 3 things you do to take care of it.	**1.** ______ **2.** ______ **3.** ______

兩人一組，詢問下方的問題，猜猜你的搭檔養什麼寵物。

 **What is your pet like?**

 My pet is cute, funny, and playful.

 **How do you take care of it?**

 I have to clean its litter box twice a week, play with it often, and brush its fur regularly.

 **Do you have a cat?**

 Yes, I do.

Unit 08 An Accident!
意外！

Warm Up

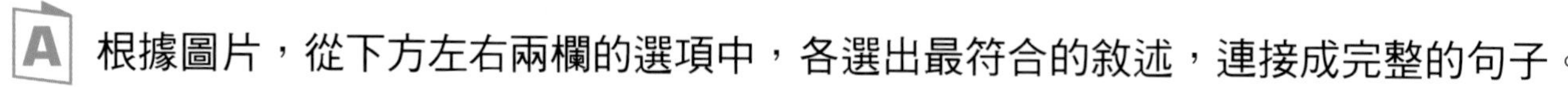

A 根據圖片，從下方左右兩欄的選項中，各選出最符合的敘述，連接成完整的句子。

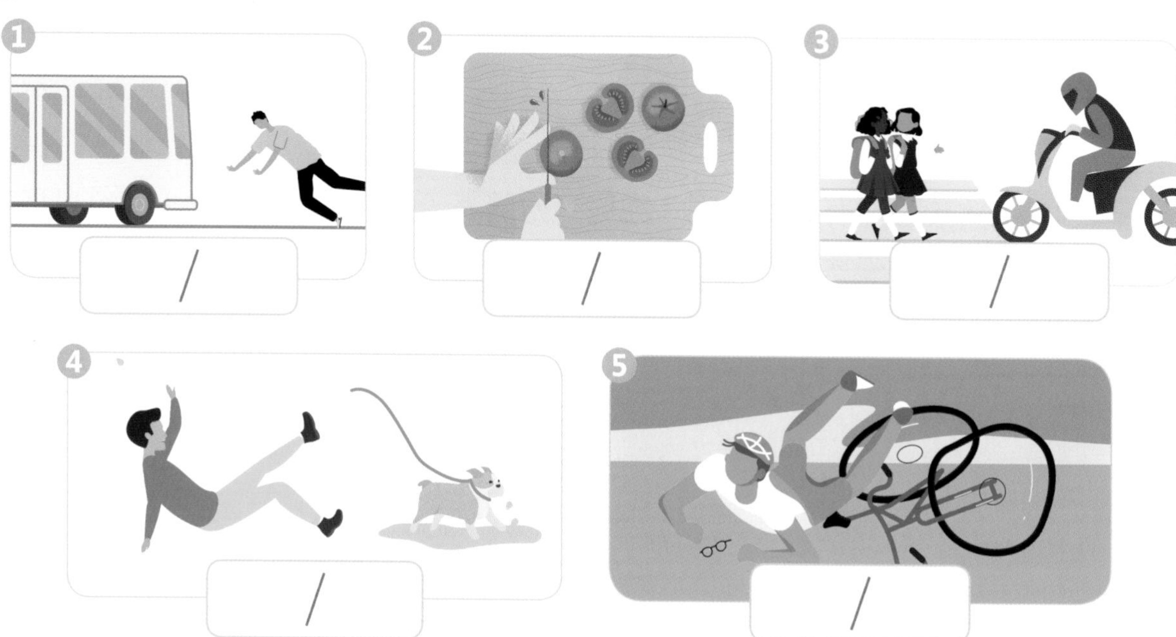

Ⓐ I cut myself	ⓐ while I was cycling by the river
Ⓑ I fell over	ⓑ while I was chopping vegetables
Ⓒ I slipped	ⓒ while I was walking my dog
Ⓓ I got hit by a scooter	ⓓ while I was running for the bus
Ⓔ I fell off my bike	ⓔ while I was crossing the road

B Pair Work 兩人一組，使用上方的連接完成的完整句練習對話。

 Oh! Are you OK?

 No, I had an accident.

 What happened?

 I cut myself while I was chopping vegetables.

Speak & Listen

A Pair Work 連連看，將受傷的原因與結果配對。

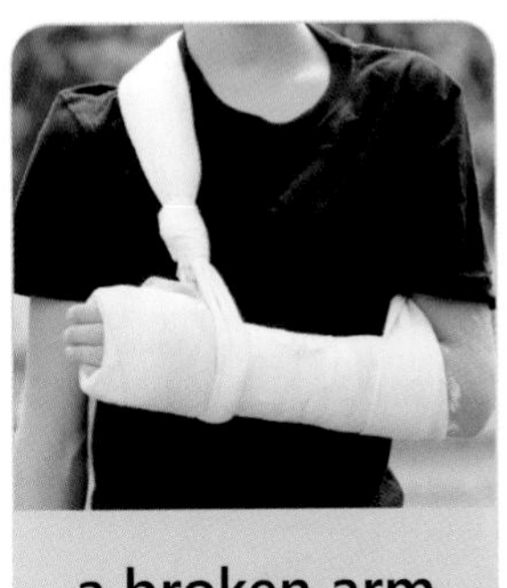

a broken arm

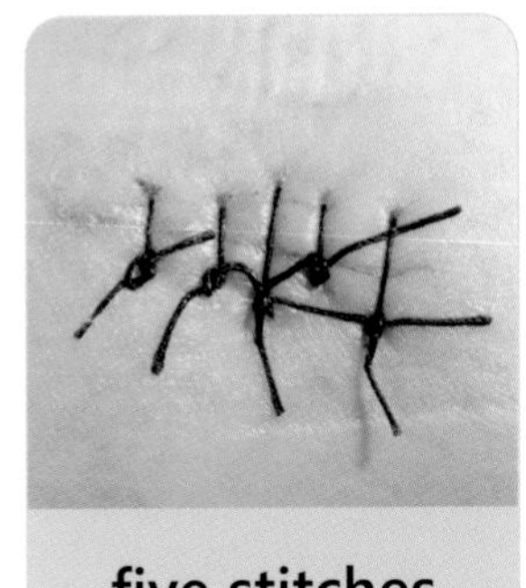

five stitches

a sprained ankle

a black eye

slipped	fell over	fell off my bike	got hit by a scooter

兩人一組，練習下列的對話。

Oh ! What happened to you?

I had an accident, so now I have a broken arm.

How did you do that?

I fell over while I was playing basketball.

15 B 李歐（Leo）在學校出了意外。聆聽他與學校護士的對話，完成護士的意外事件報告。

Student Accident Report

Name: *Leo Green*

Injury: ____________________

Cause: *hit in the face by a baseball while*____________

Does the student need to go to hospital? ☐ Yes ☐ No

If no, how did you treat the injury?

____

08 An Accident! 意外！

Dialogue

16 A 聆聽並複誦對話。

Oh! What happened to you?

I ❶ hit my head while I was playing during recess.

How did you do that?

I ❷ slipped on the wet floor.

Did you have to go to the hospital?

❸ No, the school nurse put some ice on it.

B **Pair Work** 兩人一組，將上方對話畫底線的部分，替換成下方的詞組，並進行練習。

❶ cut myself / helping my mom make dinner
❷ wasn't paying attention and the knife slipped
❸ Yes, the doctor gave me three stitches.

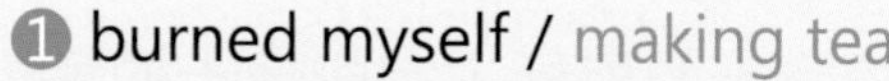
❶ burned myself / making tea
❷ touched the hot kettle
❸ No, my mom put some ointment on it.

❶ broke my finger / playing soccer
❷ I tripped over my shoelaces
❸ Yes, they gave me an X-ray and then put my finger in plaster.

Communicate

A Pair Work 回想你曾發生的意外，完成表格。

What happened to you?	*(e.g., I cut my knee while I was playing at recess.)*
How did you do that?	*(e.g., I was running and I fell over.)*
Who took care of you?	*(e.g., The school nurse.)*
How did they make it better?	*(e.g., She put a Band-Aid on it.)*

兩人一組，根據表格詢問與回答問題。

 What happened to you?

 I cut my knee while I was playing at recess.

 How did you do that?

 I was running and I fell over.

 Who took care of you?

 The school nurse took care of me.

 How did they make it better?

 She put a Band-Aid on it.

B Share With the Class 向全班分享你的搭檔發生過的意外。

 Jack cut his knee while he was playing at recess. He was running and he fell over. The school nurse took care of him and put a Band-Aid on it.

Unit 09 What Do You Want to Be? 你的志向是什麼？

Warm Up

 將下列兩個框中的職稱及敘述，與圖片配對。

1  ____ / ____

2  ____ / ____

3  ____ / ____

4  ____ / ____

5  ____ / ____

6  ____ / ____

7  ____ / ____

8  ____ / ____

Ⓐ doctor　Ⓑ teacher　Ⓒ police officer　Ⓓ athlete
Ⓔ programmer　Ⓕ artist　Ⓖ actor　Ⓗ social media influencer

Ⓘ I love computers.
Ⓙ I want to be in movies.
Ⓚ I like teaching people new things.
Ⓛ I love painting.
Ⓜ I want to protect people.
Ⓝ I love sports.
Ⓞ I love posting videos online.
Ⓟ I want to help sick people.

 **Pair Work** 兩人一組，使用上方的職稱與句子練習對話。

 What do you want to be when you grow up?

 I want to be an artist.

 Why an artist?

 Because I love painting.

Speak & Listen

A Pair Work 連連看，將職稱與它適合的技能配對。

doctor	athlete	artist	teacher

have lots of interesting new ideas

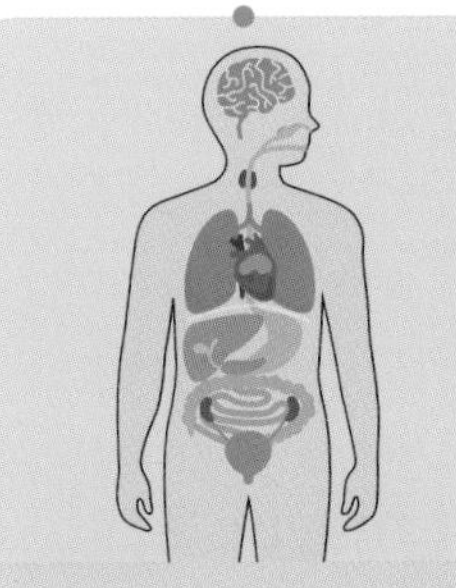
understand the human body

be able to explain difficult things clearly

exercise a lot

兩人一組，運用上方的內容練習對話。

 What do you want to be when you grow up?

 I want to be an actor.

 Is it hard to become an actor?

 Yes, you need to be very passionate about acting.

17 **B** 聆聽梅爾（Mel）與傑克（Jack）的對話，並完成下方表格。

Who?	Mel	Jack
What does he/ she want to be?	________	________
Why?	wants to keep people ________	wants to make ________
What skill does he/she need?	remember lots of different ________ / be very ________	be very good at ________

Dialogue

18 **A** 聆聽並複誦對話。

 What do you want to do after you leave school?

 I'm not sure.

 Well, what ❶ do you like doing most?

 ❷ I love helping people.

 Then how about ❸ a doctor or maybe a nurse?

 Being ❹ a doctor sounds cool. But you need to be very good at understanding the human body.

 That's OK. If you work hard, I'm sure you can learn!

 **Pair Work** 兩人一組，將上方對話畫底線的部分，替換成下方的詞組，並進行練習。

❶ are you good at
❷ I'm good at cooking
❸ a chef / a baker
❹ a chef / be able to use a knife very well

❶ are you passionate about
❷ I'm really passionate about drawing
❸ an art teacher / a fashion designer
❹ a fashion designer / know a lot about clothes

❶ are you interested in
❷ I'm really interested in nature
❸ a park ranger / a scientist
❹ a scientist / remember a lot of difficult facts

Communicate

Pair Work 先自己回答表格中的問題，再詢問你的搭檔，並寫下他的答案。

Question	My Answer	My Partner's Answer
What do you like to do in your free time?		
What is your favorite subject in school?		
Describe yourself in three words.		
What are you passionate about / interested in?		
What are you good at? What special skills do you have?		

Share With the Class 根據搭檔的答案，建議他可以從事的工作。

I think Nick would be a good English teacher because he's very patient, his favorite subject is English, and he can remember a lot of difficult English words . . .

聽搭檔給你的建議，說說你是否贊同。

Nick thinks I would be a good soccer player because I love to play soccer in my free time. But in fact I want to be a singer because I'm passionate about music . . .

Unit 10

What's the Weather Like in Your Country?

你國家的天氣怎麼樣？

Warm Up

將圖片與詞彙配對。

hot windy warm sunny cold snowy rainy cool

1

____

2

____

3

____

4

____

5

____

6

____

7

____

8

____

使用上方詞彙，形容你居住的地方的四季氣候。

spring

summer

fall

winter

 **Pair Work** 兩人一組，使用前頁的內容練習對話。

 What's summer like where you live?

 Summer is hot and windy. What's fall like where you live?

 Fall is warm and rainy.

Speak & Listen

 **Pair Work** 兩人一組，從下方選一個國家出來，利用那個國家的四季氣候字詞，套入下方會話中畫底線的色字，並練習對話。

The UK

Spring: cold, rainy
Summer: sunny, warm
Fall: rainy, windy
Winter: cold, snowy

Japan

Spring: warm, sunny
Summer: hot, rainy
Fall: warm, rainy
Winter: cold, sunny

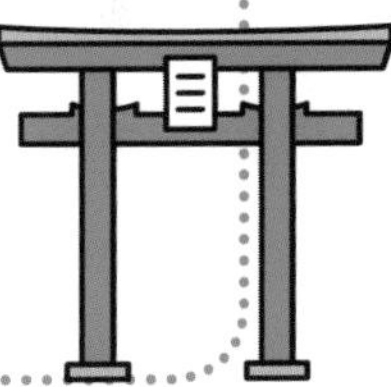

Australia

Spring: warm, sunny
Summer: hot, sunny
Fall: cool, sunny
Winter: cool, rainy

Thailand

Spring: hot, sunny
Summer: hot, rainy
Fall: hot, rainy
Winter: cool, sunny

 Where are you from?

 I'm from the UK.

 What's the weather like there?

 Spring is cold and rainy, summer is sunny and warm, fall is rainy and windy, and winter is cold and snowy.

 What's the best time to visit?

 The best time to visit the UK is summer.

19 **B** 聆聽玫（Mei）與巴比（Bobby）的對話，選出正確的答案。

____ **1.** Where is Bobby from?
ⓐ Italy　ⓑ The UK　ⓒ Korea　ⓓ The USA

____ **2.** What's the best time to visit Bobby's country?
ⓐ Fall　ⓑ Summer　ⓒ Winter　ⓓ Spring

____ **3.** What's the weather like there at that time of year?
ⓐ Warm and sunny　ⓑ Cold and sunny
ⓒ Warm and rainy　ⓓ Hot and sunny

____ **4.** What's the weather like there in summer?
ⓐ Cool and rainy　ⓑ Hot and sunny
ⓒ Warm and sunny　ⓓ Hot and rainy

Dialogue

20 **A** 聆聽並複誦對話。

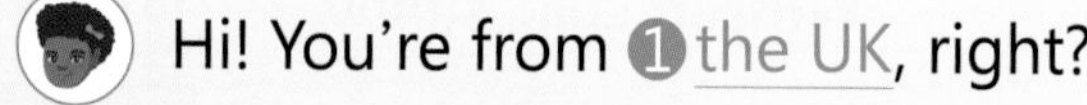

Hi! You're from ❶ the UK, right?

Yes, I am. Why do you ask?

I'm going there on vacation next year.

Oh, great! What time of year are you going?

I'm going in ❷ spring. What's the weather usually like then?

It's ❸ quite cold and it rains a lot. You should take ❹ a raincoat and some warm clothes.

I will! Thanks for the advice!

B **Pair Work** 兩人一組，將上方對話畫底線的部分，替換成下方的詞組，並進行練習。

❶ Australia
❷ summer
❸ really hot / the sun is very strong
❹ your sunglasses and lots of sunscreen

1. Taiwan
2. fall
3. nice and cool / the sun is usually shining
4. light sweater and a sun hat

1. Korea
2. winter
3. really cold / it usually snows
4. a thick coat and some gloves

Communicate

Pair Work 想想在出國前要打包什麼服飾配件，並完成表格。

Country: ____________________

Season	Clothes/Items
Spring	
Summer	
Fall	
Winter	

兩人一組，根據上方表格練習對話。

 Where are you from?

 I'm from Taiwan.

 When is the best time to visit Taiwan?

 I think the best time to visit Taiwan is spring.

 What's the weather like there in spring?

 It's warm and sunny.

 What should I pack when I visit?

 You should pack a T-shirt, shorts, and a sun hat.

Unit 11

How Will We Get There?
我們要如何到達那裡？

Warm Up

A 將圖片與詞彙配對。

1 

2 

3 

4 

5 

6 

ⓐ toy fair ⓑ museum ⓒ amusement park
ⓓ flea market ⓔ department store ⓕ ball game

B **Pair Work** 兩人一組，使用上方的詞彙，與下方的交通方式練習對話。

take a taxi | take the bus | take the train | take the subway | walk

What are you doing this weekend?

I'm going to an amusement park. Do you want to come?

I'd love to! How will we get there?

We can take the train.

Speak & Listen

Pair Work 兩人一組，選出週末想去的地方，並利用資訊練習對話。

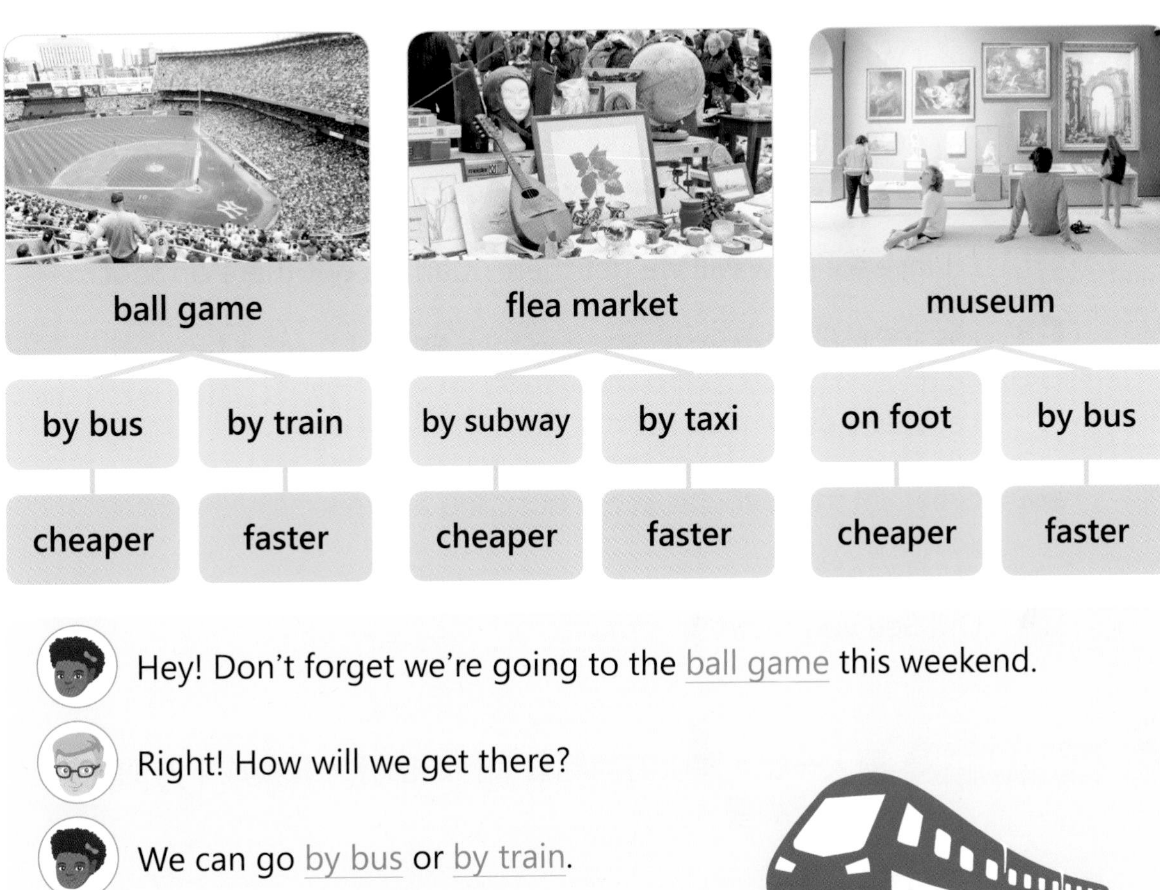

Hey! Don't forget we're going to the ball game this weekend.

Right! How will we get there?

We can go by bus or by train.

Let's go by train. It's faster.

21 **B** 聆聽艾比（Abby）與李（Lee）的對話，圈出題目中正確的字詞。

1. Abby and Lee are going to the toy fair / amusement park this weekend.
2. Lee's father can / can't take them.
3. In the end they decide to take the train / taxi because it's faster / cheaper.
4. Abby will meet Lee at the station / Lee's house at 10 o'clock on Saturday / Sunday.

11 How Will We Get There? 我們要如何到達那裡？

Dialogue

22 A 聆聽並複誦對話。

Hey! What are you doing this weekend?

I'm going to ❶the National Palace Museum. ❷It's the most famous museum in Taiwan. Do you want to come?

I'd love to! How will we get there? Can we get there on foot?

No, it's too far to walk. We can take ❸the bus or a taxi.

Let's take ❹the bus. It's cheaper.

Great. I'll meet you at ❺the bus stop at nine thirty Saturday morning.

OK! See you there.

B **Pair Work** 兩人一組，將上方對話畫底線的部分，替換成下方的詞組，並進行練習。

❶ a flea market
❷ I want to buy some interesting old things
❸ the subway / the bus ❹ the subway / faster
❺ the subway station / eight o'clock Sunday morning

❶ a ball game
❷ The Elephants are playing the Monkeys
❸ the train / a taxi ❹ the train / cheaper
❺ the train station / five o'clock Saturday evening

❶ the 5th Street Department Store
❷ I want to go shopping for some new clothes
❸ the subway / a taxi ❹ a taxi / more comfortable
❺ my house / midday tomorrow

Communicate

 **Pair Work** 兩人一組，計劃你們的週末。詢問並回答下方的問題，將你們的答案填入表格內。

Where do you want to go on ________?	Let's go to ____________.
How will we get there?	We can take the ________.
When and where shall we meet?	Let's meet at ________ at ________.

Our Weekend

	Saturday	Sunday
Where are you going?		
How are you getting there?		
Where/When are you meeting?		

 **Share With the Class** 向全班分享你和搭檔週末要做的事情。

Example

On Saturday, we're going to an amusement park. **We're going to** take the train **there. We're going to meet at the** train station **at** 9 o'clock in the morning.

On Sunday, we're going to . . .

Unit 12

Good Manners 有禮貌

Warm Up

將圖片與敘述配對，以完成句子。

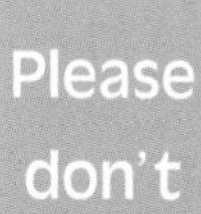

Please don't

You should

ⓐ spit on the ground.
ⓑ throw your trash on the ground.
ⓒ cut in line.
ⓓ stop in the middle of the sidewalk.
ⓔ cough everywhere.
ⓕ put it into a trash can.
ⓖ wait your turn.
ⓗ wear a mask.
ⓘ do it into a tissue.
ⓙ step to the side.

Pair Work 兩人一組，使用上方的詞語練習對話。

 Excuse me.

 Yes?

 Please don't spit on the floor.

 Oh, I'm sorry.

 You should do it into a tissue.

Speak & Listen

A **Pair Work** 兩人一組，想想面對對方的藉口時，你可以怎麼回覆。

Excuse	Reply
I don't have a mask.	*You can buy masks at a pharmacy.*
I don't know where the line starts.	
I couldn't find a trash can.	
I don't have a tissue.	
I'm lost.	

運用前頁的敘述與上方的回覆內容練習對話。

Excuse me.

Yes?

Please don't cough everywhere.
You should wear a mask.

Oh, I'm sorry.
I don't have a mask.

You can buy masks at a pharmacy.

23 B 聆聽李奇（Rich）與茉莉（Molly）的對話，根據對話內容勾選正確的答案，以完成句子。

Rich saw
- ☐ a man spitting on the street.
- ☐ a man cutting in line.
- ☐ a man throwing trash on the ground.

Rich told the man to
- ☐ put it in a trash can.
- ☐ take it home with him.
- ☐ leave it on the ground.

The man said

- ☐ he dropped it by mistake.
- ☐ he couldn't find a trash can.
- ☐ it wasn't his trash.

Rich told the man

- ☐ where he could find a trash can.
- ☐ he would call the police.
- ☐ he would help him throw away his trash.

Dialogue

24 **A** 聆聽並複誦對話。

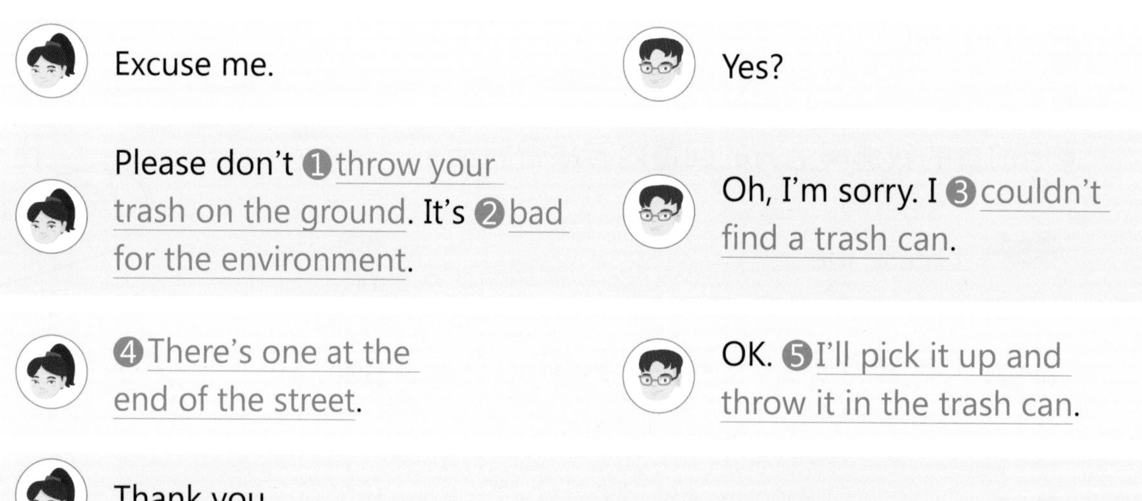

Excuse me.

Yes?

Please don't ❶ throw your trash on the ground. It's ❷ bad for the environment.

Oh, I'm sorry. I ❸ couldn't find a trash can.

❹ There's one at the end of the street.

OK. ❺ I'll pick it up and throw it in the trash can.

Thank you.

B **Pair Work** 兩人一組，將上方對話畫底線的部分，替換成下方的詞組，並進行練習。

❶ pick up the cakes with your hands
❷ unhygienic
❸ I couldn't find any tongs
❹ There are some next to the door
❺ I'll go and grab a pair

❶ run in the hallway
❷ dangerous
❸ wasn't thinking
❹ You could really hurt someone
❺ I'll walk from now on

❶ play with your phone while we're talking
❷ rude
❸ got a message from my friend
❹ You can reply to them later
❺ I'll put my phone away

Communicate

 Pair Work 兩人一組，完成表格。

Please don't . . .	Why not?	Excuse
e.g., spit on the ground.	*e.g., It's unhygienic.*	*e.g., I don't have a tissue.*

Reply	Conclusion
e.g., Here, I can give you one.	*e.g., Thank you. I'll use a tissue in the future.*

與搭檔角色模擬，用上方內容練習對話。

 Excuse me.

 Yes?

 Please don't spit on the ground.

 Why not?

 It's unhygienic.

 Sorry, I don't have a tissue.

 Here, I can give you one.

 Thank you. I'll use a tissue in the future.

 Share With the Class 兩人一組，向全班分享你們的對話內容。

 I saw John spitting on the ground. I told him to stop because it was unhygienic.

 I said I didn't have a tissue.

 So I said I could give him one.

 In the end I said thank you, I would use a tissue in the future.

Unit 13

A Surprise
驚喜

Warm Up

根據人物的描述，選出最適合他們的禮物。

1 

2 

3 

4 

5 

6 

a 
notebook

b 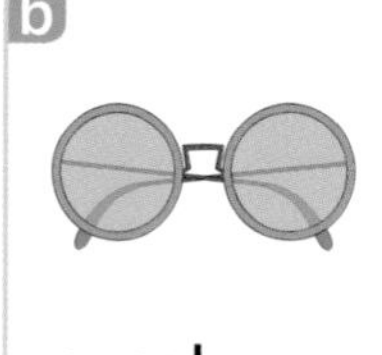
sunglasses

c 
earphones

d 
scarf

e 
phone case

f 

jersey

B **Pair Work** 兩人一組，使用上方的人物描述與詞彙練習對話。

 Happy birthday, Jenny!

 Wow! New earphones!

 I know how much you like listening to music.

 Thank you so much!

Speak & Listen

Pair Work 根據下方人物的敘述，寫下你認為最適合他們的禮物。

Max

I like to play soccer and listen to music.

Gift for Max: ______________________

Mia

I like to write stories and read comic books.

Gift for Mia: ______________________

Jack

I like to paint and wear cool clothes.

Gift for Jack: ______________________

兩人一組，使用上方內容練習對話。

What do you think Max would like for his birthday?

I think he'd like ______________ because ______________.

25 **B** 特洛伊（Troy）與吉娜（Gina）在討論要送給朋友丹（Dan）的生日禮物。聆聽他們的對話，勾選出他們最終要送的禮物。

☐ 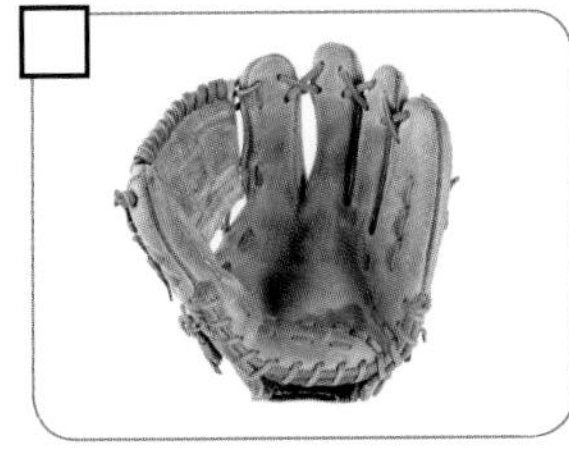

☐ 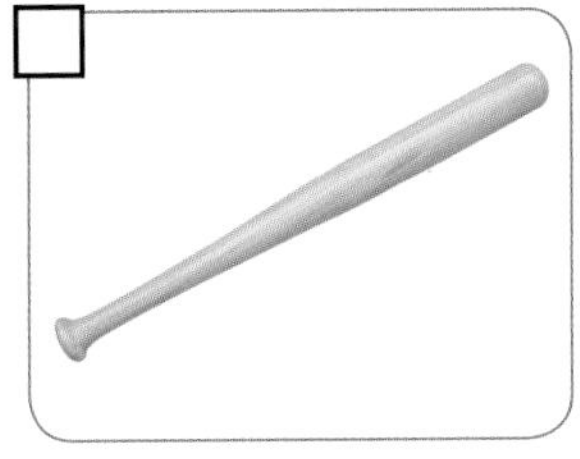

☐ 

☐ 

13 A Surprise 驚喜

Dialogue

 26 A 聆聽並複誦對話。

 What are you buying Mike for his birthday?

 I'm buying him ❶ a soccer jersey because I know how much he likes soccer.

 That sounds like a great gift. What else does he like?

 He also likes ❷ music.

 Maybe I could buy him ❸ some earphones.

 Great idea. I'm sure he'd love that!

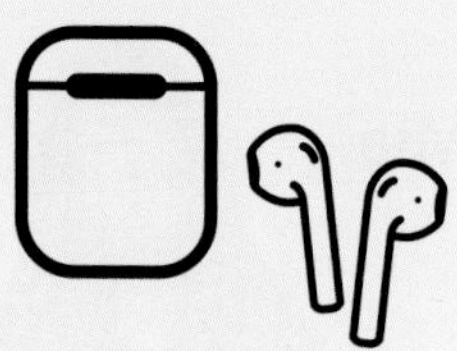

 **Pair Work** 兩人一組，將上方對話畫底線的部分，替換成下方的詞組，並進行練習。

❶ a paint brush / painting
❷ running
❸ running shoes

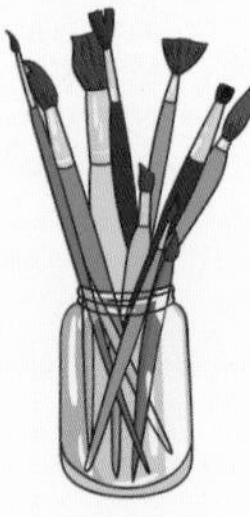

❶ a model airplane / planes
❷ swimming
❸ swimming goggles

❶ a comic book / comics
❷ movies
❸ a movie poster

Communicate

Group Work 三人一組，學生 A 與 B 利用下方對話，討論要送給 C 的生日禮物。可參考下方的補充詞彙。

 What do you think Kat would like for her birthday?

 I know she likes movies. Maybe we could buy her a movie poster.

 That's a great idea! I'm sure she'd love that.

利用下方對話，給學生 C 一個驚喜的生日禮物。

  Happy birthday, Kat!

 Thanks, Max! Thanks Rachel!

 Rachel and I have a gift for you.
We know how much you like movies.

 Wow! A movie poster! Thank you!

  You're welcome!

重複練習這個活動，讓學生 A、B 與 C 都收到禮物。

Extra Vocabulary

cake 蛋糕	**trading cards** 卡牌	**board game** 桌遊	**wallet** 皮夾	**ukulele** 烏克麗麗

Unit 14

What's Cooking?

你在做什麼？

Warm Up

A 看看下方的菜餚與甜點，如果烹煮（cook）出來的就寫「C」，是烘焙（bake）出來的就寫「B」。

B Pair Work 兩人一組，使用上方的詞彙練習對話。

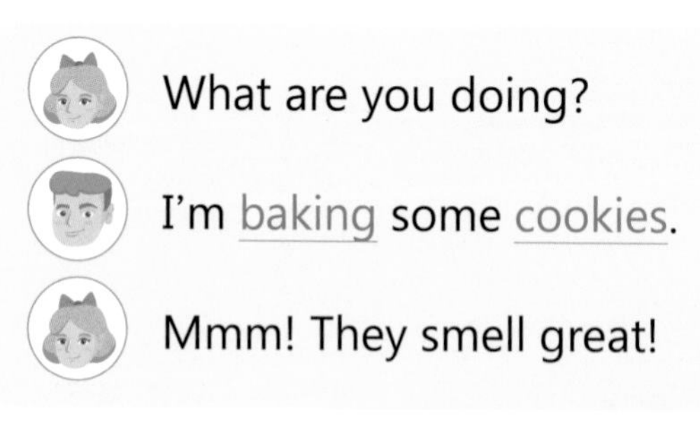

What are you doing?

I'm baking some cookies.

Mmm! They smell great!

Speak & Listen

 **Pair Work** 連連看，將甜點與口味配對。

兩人一組，利用配對內容練習對話。

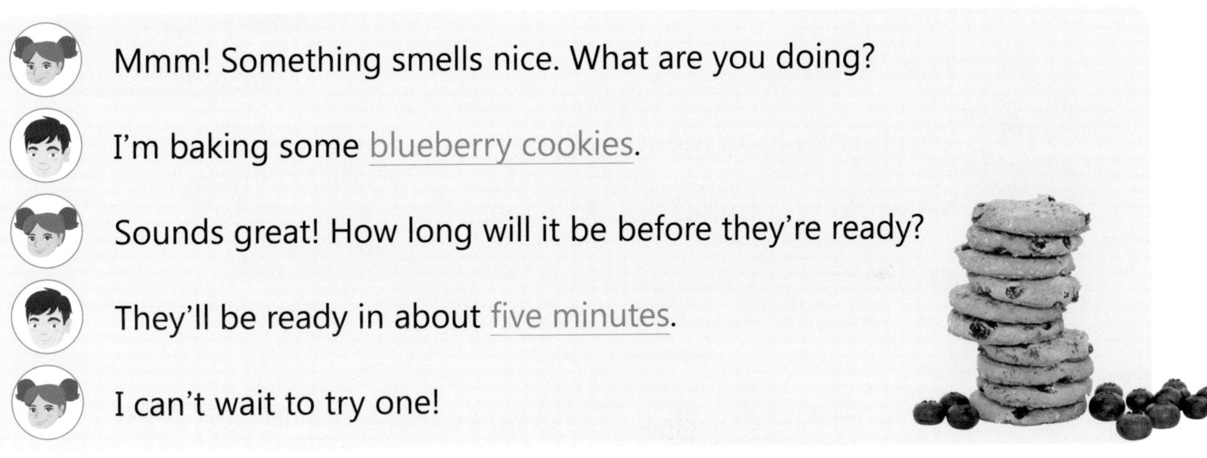

Mmm! Something smells nice. What are you doing?

I'm baking some blueberry cookies.

Sounds great! How long will it be before they're ready?

They'll be ready in about five minutes.

I can't wait to try one!

27 **B** 聆聽凱（Kay）與她父親的對話，正確的選 **T**，錯誤的選 **F**。

1. Kay's father is making blueberry muffins. T / F
2. Kay's father says the muffins will be ready in 30 minutes. T / F
3. Kay's father is afraid the muffins are too sour. T / F
4. Kay thinks the muffins taste delicious. T / F
5. Kay's father says she can eat them all by herself. T / F

Dialogue

28 **A** 聆聽並複誦對話。

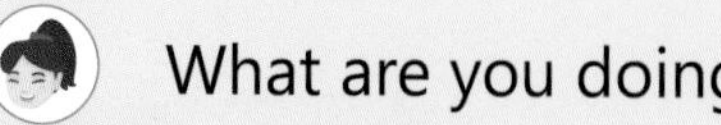

What are you doing?

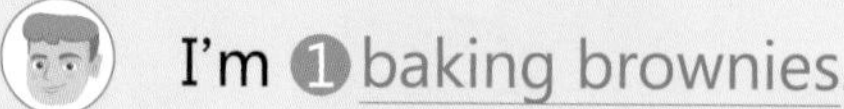

I'm ❶ baking brownies.

Ooh! What kind?

❷ Peanut butter and banana.

My favorite! How long will it be before they're ready?

Around five minutes.

Great! I can't wait to try one.

[Later . . .]

They're ready!

Wow! They look great!

What do you think? Too ❸ sweet?

❹ No, they're really delicious.

B **Pair Work** 兩人一組，將上方對話畫底線的部分，替換成下方的詞組，並進行練習。

❶ baking scones
❷ chocolate chip
❸ bland
❹ A little. I think they need a bit more sugar.

❶ cooking dumplings
❷ pork
❸ salty
❹ No, it's just right.

❶ baking some tarts
❷ apple
❸ sour
❹ A tiny bit, but I think it would taste great with some ice cream.

Communicate

Pair Work 想想你想要烹煮或烘焙的食物，並完成表格。

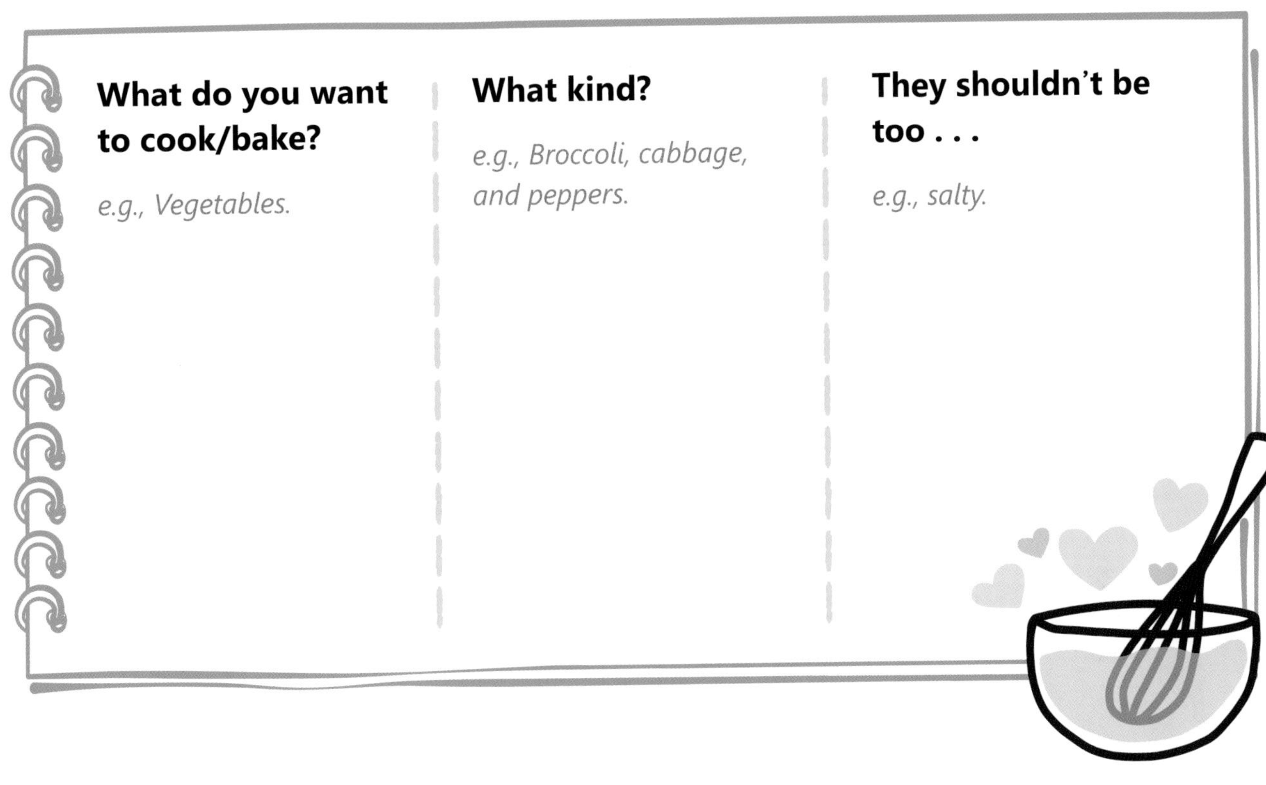

What do you want to cook/bake?	What kind?	They shouldn't be too . . .
e.g., Vegetables.	*e.g., Broccoli, cabbage, and peppers.*	*e.g., salty.*

兩人一組，使用上方的表格練習對話。

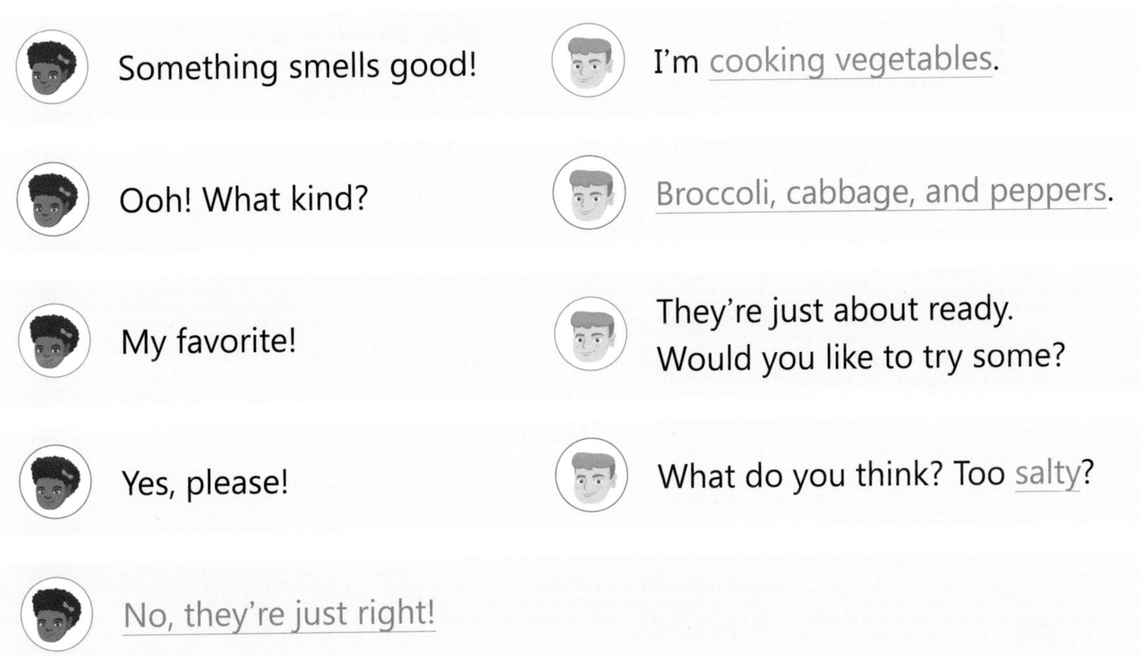

Something smells good!

I'm cooking vegetables.

Ooh! What kind?

Broccoli, cabbage, and peppers.

My favorite!

They're just about ready.
Would you like to try some?

Yes, please!

What do you think? Too salty?

No, they're just right!

Unit 15

What Do You Do After School? 你放學後會做什麼？

Warm Up

配對圖片與敘述。

1 

2 

3 

4 

5 

6 

7 

8 

9 

10 

ⓐ have dinner
ⓑ do chores
ⓒ practice dancing
ⓓ do homework
ⓔ go to bed
ⓕ play video games
ⓖ take a shower
ⓗ go on social media
ⓘ read
ⓙ practice piano

Pair Work 兩人一組，利用上方敘述練習對話。

What do you do when you get home from school?

I have dinner, do chores, do homework, take a shower, and then go to bed.

Speak & Listen

 **Pair Work** 兩人一組，根據班（Ben）和茱莉亞（Julia）的課後例常行程練習對話。

 What does Ben do after dinner?

 After dinner, he ____________.

 How long does that usually take him?

 It usually takes him about ____________.

 What does he do after that?

 After that he ____________.

 How much time does he spend doing that?

 He spends about ____________ doing that.

 What does he do after ________?

 After ____________, he ____________.

29 **B** 聆聽提姆（Tim）與珍（Jen）的對話，將珍放學後的行程填入表格。

Jen

5:00 p.m.	6:00 p.m.		7:30 p.m.		9:30 p.m.	
eat dinner		go on social media		take a shower		go to bed

Dialogue

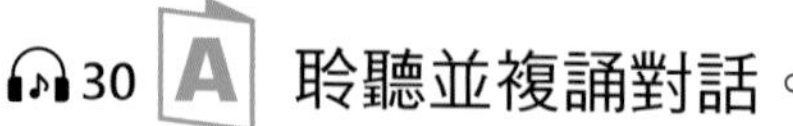

30 **A** 聆聽並複誦對話。

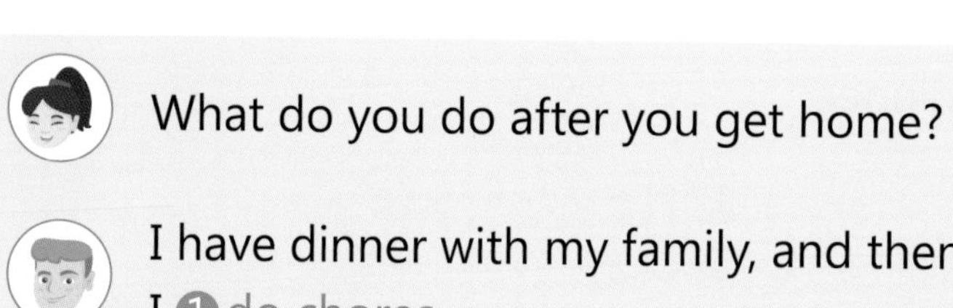

What do you do after you get home?

I have dinner with my family, and then I ❶ do chores.

How long does that take you?

It takes me around ❷ thirty minutes.

And after that, what do you do?

Then I take a break and ❸ read some comic books.

How much time do you spend doing that?

About an hour. And then I ❹ do homework until 9 p.m.

What time do you go to bed?

I'm usually in bed by 10 p.m. every night.

兩人一組，將上方對話畫底線的部分，替換成下方的詞組，並進行練習。

➊ practice violin
➋ an hour

➌ watch a TV show

➍ have an art lesson

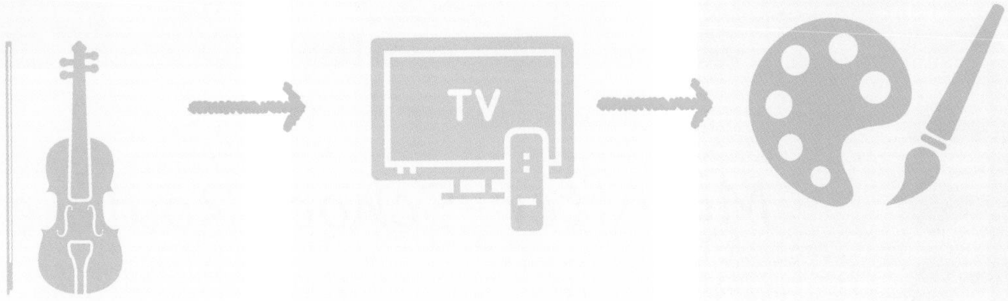

➊ review what I learned in school
➋ forty-five minutes

➌ play some games on my phone

➍ practice calligraphy

➊ walk the dog
➋ twenty minutes

➌ listen to some music

➍ study for any upcoming tests

Communicate

 Pair Work 你放學後都做些什麼呢？寫下你的例常行程。

My After-School Routine

Activity	Duration
e.g., have dinner with my parents	e.g., 1 hour
____________________	________
____________________	________
____________________	________
____________________	________
____________________	________
____________________	________

Bedtime: ____________

兩人一組，利用前頁的行程練習對話。

 What do you do after school?

 I have dinner with my parents.

 How long does that take?

 About an hour.

 And after that?

 After that I ________________.

 And then?

 Then I ________________. And I'm usually in bed by ______.

 **Share With the Class** 向全班分享，你和搭檔行程的異同處。

 **I spend** an hour doing my homework**, but** Ben **only spends** thirty minutes. We both go to bed at 10 o'clock.

Unit 16

Save the Planet 守護地球

Warm Up

配對圖片與敘述。

1 

2 

3 

4 

5 

Ⓐ Don't waste water. Ⓑ Don't waste electricity.
Ⓒ Don't buy plastic bags. Ⓓ Don't use plastic straws. Ⓔ Don't waste paper.

B 連連看，將左欄中不該做的事，與右欄中的正確行為配對。

Don't . . .	You should . . .
waste water •	• use a metal one
waste electricity •	• write on both sides
buy plastic bags •	• turn off the lights when you are leaving a room
use plastic straws •	• bring your own cloth one
waste paper •	• turn off the tap when you're brushing your teeth

Pair Work 兩人一組，使用上方配對的內容練習對話。

You know, you really shouldn't use plastic straws.

What's the problem?

It's bad for the planet. You should ________________.

Speak & Listen

A Pair Work 下方是會破壞地球的行為，想想我們應該如何行動，來避免這些行為。

⊘ keep the AC on all night	⊘ go everywhere by car	⊘ use disposable chopsticks	⊘ use paper cups
✓ turn it off after one hour, use a fan	✓ ____________	✓ ____________	✓ ____________

兩人一組，分享彼此的想法。

People really shouldn't keep the AC on all night. They should turn it off after one hour.

I agree. Or they could also use a fan.

31 B 聆聽羅伯（Rob）與朵拉（Dora）的對話，根據上半句的內容，勾選出正確的下半句。

1. You really shouldn't . . .

- ☐ go everywhere by car.
- ☐ use paper cups.
- ☐ waste water.

2. You should use . . .

- ☐ a water bottle.
- ☐ a plate.
- ☐ a metal one.

3. If everyone just helps a little, we can . . .

- ☐ stop wasting so much paper.
- ☐ save a lot of water.
- ☐ make our planet much cleaner.

4. Thanks for . . .

- ☐ helping the planet.
- ☐ changing your mind.
- ☐ being nice.

Dialogue

32 **A** 聆聽並複誦對話。

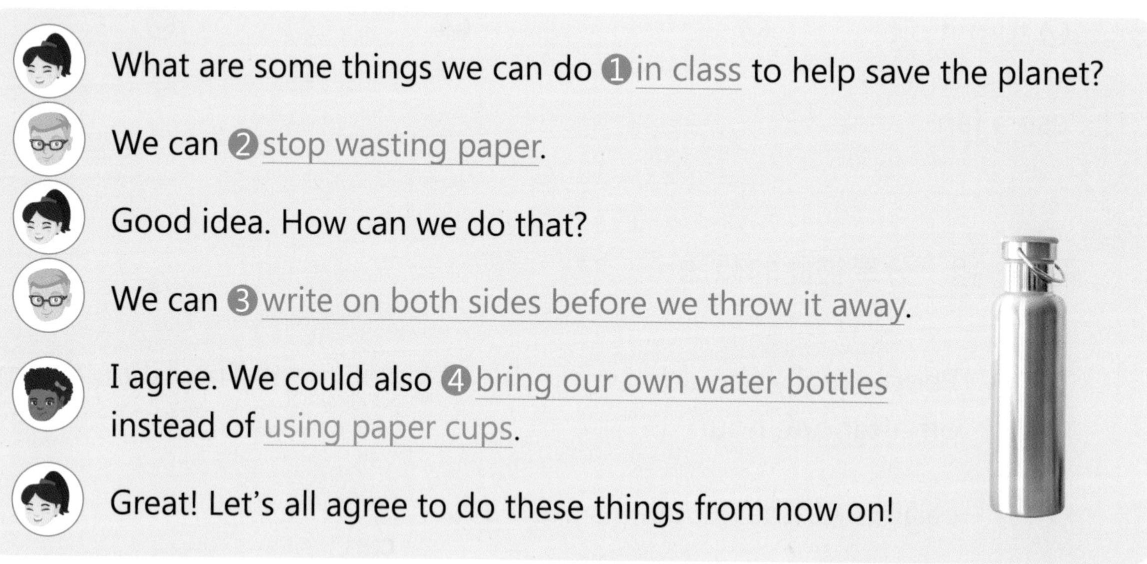

What are some things we can do ❶ in class to help save the planet?

We can ❷ stop wasting paper.

Good idea. How can we do that?

We can ❸ write on both sides before we throw it away.

I agree. We could also ❹ bring our own water bottles instead of using paper cups.

Great! Let's all agree to do these things from now on!

B **Group Work** 三人一組，將上方對話畫底線的部分，替換成下方的詞組，並進行練習。

❶ at home
❷ use less water
❸ turn off the tap while brushing our teeth
❹ take a shower / having a bath

❶ while shopping
❷ use less plastic
❸ avoid buying things that are wrapped in plastic
❹ bring our own cloth bag / buying a plastic one

1 at dinnertime
2 waste less
3 use our leftovers for lunch the next day
4 use metal chopsticks / disposable ones

Communicate

A Group Work 在學校可以怎麼做來保護地球？四人一組，舉出五個例子。

1. ____________________
2. ____________________
3. ____________________
4. ____________________
5. ____________________

B Share With the Class 將你們的想法告訴全班同學。當其他同學在報告時，記得仔細聆聽。

To help save the planet, we think we can . . .

C Class Discussion 討論出五個你們覺得最棒的點子，填入下方表格中。

To help save the planet, our class will . . .

1. ____________________
2. ____________________
3. ____________________
4. ____________________
5. ____________________

Answer Key
&
Scripts & Translation

Unit 01 First Day at School 開學日

Warm Up

A P. 10

1 f　2 e　3 i　4 k
5 l　6 b　7 j　8 d
9 a　10 g　11 h　12 c

Speak & Listen

B 01 P. 11

1 a　2 b　3 b　4 c

Lilly: Hi, I'm Lilly. What's your name?
Ben: Hi, I'm Ben.
Lilly: Are you a new student?
Ben: Yes, I'm in grade 7. What grade are you in?
Lilly: I'm in grade 8. What class are you in?
Ben: I'm in class 101.
Lilly: My sister is in that class, too. She's your classmate. Her name is Laura.
Ben: Oh! I know her. She sits next to me.
Lilly: Do you like your homeroom teacher?
Ben: Yes, Mr. Rees is very nice.
Lilly: That's great! Oh, sorry, I have to run. But it was nice talking to you. Welcome to our school!
Ben: Thanks! See you later.

莉莉：嗨，我是莉莉，你叫什麼名字？
班：嗨，我是班。
莉莉：你是新同學嗎？
班：是，我七年級。你幾年級？
莉莉：我八年級。你在哪一班？
班：我在 101 班。
莉莉：我妹也在那一班，她是你的同學，她的名字叫蘿拉。
班：喔！我知道她，她坐在我隔壁。
莉莉：你喜歡你的班級導師嗎？
班：喜歡，力斯老師人很好。
莉莉：太好了！喔，抱歉，我得走了。很高興和你說話。歡迎來我們學校！
班：謝謝！之後見。

Dialogue

A：嗨，你也是七年級嗎？
B：是，我是。你的班級教室是哪間？
A：我是在 103 教室。你呢？
B：我在 102。你們班有很多學生嗎？
A：有，有 35 位。
B：誰是你的班級導師？
A：我的班級導師是楊老師。喔！我該去上下一堂課了！下次聊！

Unit 02 Sports Day 運動會

Warm Up

P. 14

a J　b A　c J　d J
e A　f A　g A　h J

B 03 P. 16

Who	Rich		Kate	
Event	badminton tournament	**running race**	**long jump**	ping pong tournament
Start Time	**11:00**	9:00	10:00	**2:30**

Kate: Hey, Rich. Come here. It's time to sign up for our school sports day.

Rich: Great! I want to sign up for the badminton tournament and the soccer game.

Kate: You can't do that. They both start at 11 o'clock.

Rich: Hmm. What time is the running race?

Kate: That's at 9 o'clock.

Rich: OK, then I'll sign up for the badminton tournament and the running race. How about you, Kate?

Kate: I want to sign up for the long jump. That's at 10 o'clock. And I want to sign up for the ping pong tournament at two thirty.

Rich: Awesome. I can't wait for sports day! It's going to be so much fun.

凱特： 嘿，李奇，來這邊。該報名我們學校的運動會了！

李奇： 太棒了！我想報名羽毛球聯賽跟足球比賽。

凱特： 你沒辦法辦到的，這兩個都是 11 點開始。

李奇： 跑步比賽是什麼時候啊？

凱特： 是 9 點。

李奇： 好吧，那我報名羽毛球聯賽與跑步比賽。那妳呢，凱特？

凱特： 我想要報名 10 點的跳遠。我還想報名 2 點半的乒乓球聯賽。

李奇： 讚耶。我等不及運動會了！一定會很好玩的。

A 04 P. 16

A：你目前為止在運動會還開心嗎？

B：開心，我覺得很棒。

A：你等等有任何比賽嗎？

B：有，我等等有排球比賽。

A：什麼時候啊？

B：兩點。

A：你和誰比啊？

B：我們和 106 班比。

A：祝你好運！

Unit 03 At a Restaurant 在餐廳

Warm Up

P. 20

Dino's American Restaurant			
Appetizers	Caesar **Salad**	Tomato **Soup**	**Chicken** Wings
Main Courses	**Spaghetti**	**Burger** and **Fries**	**Pizza**
Desserts	**Ice Cream**	Chocolate **Cake**	Apple **Pie**
Drinks	**Coke**	Iced **Tea**	Orange **Juice**

Speak & Listen

B 05 P. 22

Order Form
Table: 5
Appetizers: **tomato soup**
Main Courses: pizza with **cheese**, onion, and **bacon**
Desserts: ice cream—vanilla and **chocolate**
Drinks: **iced tea**

Server: Good afternoon, sir. Are you ready to order?
Customer: Yes, can I have the tomato soup to start?
Server: One tomato soup appetizer. And for your main course?
Customer: I'll have the pizza, please.
Server: Which toppings would you like on your pizza?
Customer: I think I'll have cheese, onion, and bacon.
Server: Anything for dessert?
Customer: Yes, I'll have ice cream—two scoops, please.
Server: Which flavors would you like? We have vanilla, chocolate, and strawberry.
Customer: I'll have vanilla and chocolate.
Server: And to drink?
Customer: A glass of iced tea.
Server: Great. I'll be back with your food soon.

服務生： 午安，先生。可以點餐了嗎？
顧客： 可以，可以先上番茄湯嗎？
服務生： 一碗番茄湯作開胃菜。那您的主菜呢？
顧客： 麻煩給我披薩。
服務生： 您想要放什麼配料在上面呢？
顧客： 我想要起司、洋蔥和培根。
服務生： 需要甜點嗎？
顧客： 要，麻煩給我冰淇淋，兩匙。
服務生： 您想要什麼口味？我們有香草、巧克力與草莓。
顧客： 我要香草與巧克力。
服務生： 那要喝什麼呢？
顧客： 一杯冰茶。
服務生： 好的，我會儘快送上您的餐點。

Dialogue

A 06 P. 23

A：您準備好點餐了嗎？
B：好了。可以麻煩給我牛肉麵嗎？
A：沒問題。需要飲料嗎？
B：要。綠茶。
A：熱的還是冰的呢？
B：熱的。
A：還要其他的嗎？
B：不用，這樣就好，謝謝你。

Unit 04 What Do You Like to Do in Your Free Time?
你空閒時喜歡做什麼？

Warm Up

A P. 26

James [**f**]	Charlie [**a**]	May [**c**]	Lisa [**h**]
Fred [**d**]	Joe [**b**]	Nick [**g**]	Sue [**e**]

Speak & Listen

 07 P. 28

Who?	Ray	Bella
What?	bake	read
How often?	once a week	every day
With whom?	his mom	by herself

Ray: What do you like to do in your free time, Bella?
Bella: I like to read by myself.
Ray: My brother likes to read, too. He reads every day after school.
Bella: I read every day, too. It's my favorite thing. What do you like to do in your free time, Ray?
Ray: I like to bake with my mom. We make delicious cakes together.
Bella: That sounds great! How often do you bake?
Ray: My mom is quite busy, so we can only do it once a week. I'll bring you one of our cakes sometime.
Bella: Wow! Thank you!

雷： 妳有空的時候喜歡做什麼，貝拉？
貝拉： 我喜歡獨自看書。
雷： 我弟弟也喜歡看書。他每天放學後都會看書。
貝拉： 我也每天看書。這是我最喜歡的事情。你有空的時候喜歡做什麼呢，雷？
雷： 我喜歡和我媽烘焙。我們會一起做很好吃的蛋糕。
貝拉： 聽起來好棒！你們多常烘焙？
雷： 我媽挺忙的，所以我們只能一星期一次。我下次帶我們的蛋糕來給妳。
貝拉： 哇！謝謝你！

Dialogue

 08 P. 28

A： 你空閒時間喜歡做什麼？
B： 我在家的時候喜歡拼拼圖，還有我每週打網球一次。
A： 喔，酷耶。你和教練一起打嗎？
B： 沒有，我和朋友打。
A： 聽起來很有趣。
B： 或許你下次可以加入我們！
A： 謝謝你，我很樂意！

Unit 05 Asking for Directions 問路

Warm Up

 P. 30

1 b 2 f 3 d 4 g
5 c 6 e 7 a 8 i
9 l 10 h 11 j 12 k

Speak & Listen

 09 P. 32

1 c 2 c 3 a 4 b

Max: Excuse me. I'm looking for a bookstore. Is there one near here?
Woman: Yes, there's one on Fifth Street called The Big Blue Bookstore.
Max: Fifth Street—is that far from here? Do I need to take a taxi?

Woman:	No, it's not too far. You can walk there in about five minutes.
Max:	Oh, that's great. Sorry, I'm not from around here. How do I get to Fifth Street? Could you give me some directions?
Woman:	No problem. It's quite easy. Go straight for three blocks. Then turn left. The bookstore is on your right, between the café and the museum.
Max:	That's great. Thank you so much for your help.
Woman:	You're welcome!

麥克斯： 不好意思，我在找一間書店，這附近有嗎？

女人： 有，第五街上有一間，叫做碩藍書店。

麥克斯： 第五街，離這裡遠嗎？我需要搭計程車嗎？

女人： 不用，並不會太遠。你可以走過去，五分鐘內到。

麥克斯： 喔，太好了。抱歉，我不是這裡人，我要怎麼去第五街呢？您可以給我一些指示嗎？

女人： 沒問題，很簡單的。直走三個街區，然後左轉，書店就在你的右邊，在咖啡店與博物館之間。

麥克斯： 好的。非常謝謝您的幫助。

女人： 不客氣！

Dialogue

A 🎧10 P. 33

A：不好意思，你可以幫幫我嗎？我在找市立動物園。

B：可以啊，我知道動物園，就在第二街上。

A：這麼遠嗎？我應該搭計程車嗎？

B：不用，走路只要大概 15 分鐘。

A：好的。我要怎麼從這裡去那？

B：直走三個街區，右轉。動物園就在你的左邊，在博物館旁。

A：太好了，十分感謝你的幫忙！

Unit 06 Your Summer Vacation 你的暑假

Warm Up

A P. 36

1 C / M　2 A / N　3 D / P　4 E / L

5 G / I　6 B / J　7 F / K　8 H / O

Speak & Listen

B 🎧11 P. 38

	Nick	Bea
Where?	Australia	China
With whom?	mom and older brother	whole family
What did he/ she do?	swam in the sea	ate noodles
Was it fun?	yes	no

Nick:	Hi, Bea! How was your summer vacation?
Bea:	It wasn't great.
Nick:	I'm sorry to hear that. Where did you go?
Bea:	My whole family and I went to China.

Nick: I heard China's a great place to go for a vacation. What happened?
Bea: It rained the whole time.
Nick: Oh, no! What did you do?
Bea: We just stayed inside and ate noodles. How was your summer vacation?
Nick: Mine was great. I went to Australia with my mom and older brother.
Bea: How was the weather?
Nick: It was sunny all the time. We swam in the sea every day.
Bea: You're so lucky!
Nick: Yeah, it was a lot of fun.

尼克：嗨，碧！妳的暑假過得如何？
碧：　並不是很好。
尼克：很遺憾聽到妳這麼說。妳去了哪裡呢？
碧：　我和全家人去了中國。
尼克：我聽說中國是個適合旅遊的好地方呢，發生什麼事了嗎？
碧：　一直在下雨。
尼克：喔，不！你們做了什麼？
碧：　我們就在室內吃麵囉。那你的暑假如何呢？
尼克：我過得很棒。我跟我媽和大哥去了澳洲。
碧：　天氣如何呢？
尼克：一直都是晴天呢。我們每天都在海裡游泳。
碧：　你真是幸運！
尼克：對啊，玩得很開心。

Dialogue

P. 38

A：你暑假有去什麼有趣的地方嗎？
B：有，我有。我和我家人去了英國。
A：喔，真好！我去年去過那裡。你有去參觀白金漢宮嗎？
B：有，我們有去，然後還在鄉間騎腳踏車。
A：聽起來你玩得很開心！
B：我是啊！我希望我以後還能再去那。

Unit 07 Do You Have a Pet? 你有養寵物嗎？

Warm Up

P. 42

1 dog/puppy　2 cat/kitten　3 snake
4 turtle　5 parrot　6 rabbit
7 tropical fish　8 mouse

Speak & Listen

P. 43

cat	tropical fish	parrot	dog
1. 一週清便盆兩次 **2.** 常和牠玩 **3.** 一天餵牠兩次	**1.** 一週換水一次 **2.** 一天餵牠兩次 **3.** 給牠的水缸買些植物	**1.** 一週清牠的籠子一次 **2.** 確保牠有足夠的食物與水 **3.** 常和牠說話	**1.** 每天帶牠散步 **2.** 一天餵牠兩次 **3.** 常和牠玩

P. 44

1 Jim wants to get a new ~~kitten~~ puppy.

2 Sally says Jim should feed his new pet ~~two~~ four times a day.

3 Sally says Jim should walk his new pet for a ~~long~~ **short** walk ~~once~~ **twice** a day.

4 Jim thinks that taking care of this pet will be ~~easy~~ **a lot of work**.

Jim: Hi, Sally. You have a dog, right?
Sally: Yes, I have a little puppy named Charlie.
Jim: I'm thinking about getting a puppy myself. How do you take care of one?
Sally: Well, puppies eat a lot, so you need to feed it four times a day.
Jim: That's a lot of food! How about exercise? Do puppies need to go for walks?
Sally: Yes, you have to take your puppy for a short walk twice a day.
Jim: OK. I can do that.
Sally: But remember: puppies have a lot of energy, so you have to play with it a lot at home, too.
Jim: Wow! That sounds like a lot of work.
Sally: It is, but it's worth it. You'll see.

吉姆： 嗨，莎莉，妳有養狗對嗎？
莎莉： 有，我有一隻叫做查理的小狗。
吉姆： 我在考慮要自己買隻小狗，妳是怎麼照顧小狗的呢？
莎莉： 小狗吃很多，所以你一天需要餵牠四次。
吉姆： 那吃很多耶！那運動呢？小狗需要散步嗎？
莎莉： 需要，你一天要帶小狗稍微散步兩次。
吉姆： 好，這我做得到。
莎莉： 但記得，小狗精力旺盛，所以你在家也要陪牠玩喔。
吉姆： 哇！聽起來要做好多事情。
莎莉： 對啊，但很值得，你以後就會懂。

Dialogue

A

14 P. 44

A： 你家裡有養寵物嗎？
B： 有，我有一隻兔子。
A： 牠們是怎樣的寵物啊？
B： 牠們愛玩又可愛。
A： 牠們會很難照顧嗎？
B： 你需要餵牠們很多蔬菜，還要經常梳牠們的毛。
A： 還不難呢。聽起來牠們是很好的寵物！

Unit 08 An Accident! 意外！

Warm Up

A
P. 46

1 B / d	2 A / b	3 D / e
4 C / c	5 E / a	

Speak & Listen

B

15 P. 47

Student Accident Report

Name: Leo Green
Injury: **black eye**
Cause: hit in the face by a baseball while **playing with his friends**
Does the student need to go to hospital?
☐ Yes ☑ No
If no, how did you treat the injury?
put some ice on it

Knock on the door

School Nurse:	Come in.
Leo:	Good afternoon, Nurse.
School Nurse:	Hello, Leo. My goodness, that's a big black eye you have there. How did that happen?
Leo:	I was playing with my friends and someone threw a baseball and it hit me in the face.
School Nurse:	Oh dear. Well, let me take a look. Hmm. it doesn't look too serious. You won't need to go to the hospital.
Leo:	But it really hurts!
School Nurse:	Here, let me put some ice on it. Keep that on for a few hours and it should feel better.
Leo:	Thank you, Nurse.
School Nurse:	You're welcome. Just be more careful in the future, OK?
Leo:	I will.

（敲門）

學校護士：	進來。
李歐：	午安，護士。
學校護士：	你好，李歐。天啊，你眼睛有個大淤青呢，怎麼會這樣？
李歐：	我在和我朋友玩，結果有人丟棒球砸到我的臉。
學校護士：	喔天。我來看看。恩，看起來不是很嚴重，你不需要去醫院。
李歐：	但真的很痛！
學校護士：	來，我放些冰塊上去。持續幾個小時後應該會感覺好一點。
李歐：	謝謝你，護士。
學校護士：	不客氣。以後小心一點，好嗎？
李歐：	我會的。

Dialogue

A  16 P. 48

A：喔！你發生什麼事情了？
B：我下課在玩的時候撞到我的頭。
A：你怎麼會這樣？
B：我在濕地板上滑倒了。
A：你需要去醫院嗎？
B：不用，學校護士有用冰敷了。

Unit 09 What do You Want to Be? 你的志向是什麼？

Warm Up

A P. 50

1 H / O　2 F / L　3 B / K　4 D / N
5 A / P　6 G / J　7 C / M　8 E / I

Speak & Listen

B  17 P. 51

Who?	Mel	Jack
What does he/she want to be?	**police officer**	**programmer**
Why?	wants to keep people **safe**	wants to make **computer games**
What skill does he/she need?	remember lots of different **rules** / be very **brave**	be very good at **math**

Mel: What do you want to be when you grow up, Jack?
Jack: I want to be a programmer.
Mel: Why a programmer?
Jack: I love computer games and I want to make them.
Mel: That's cool. Is it hard to become a programmer?
Jack: Yes, you need to be very good at math. That's why I study so hard in math class! How about you, Mel? What do you want to be when you grow up?
Mel: I'd like to be a police officer.
Jack: My father is a police officer. He said you have to remember a lot of different rules and also be very brave.
Mel: I think I can do that. I really want to help keep people safe.

梅爾：你長大後想做什麼，傑克？
傑克：我想當工程師。
梅爾：為什麼是工程師？
傑克：我愛電腦遊戲，我想製作它們。
梅爾：酷。成為工程師會很難嗎？
傑克：會，數學得很好才行。這就是我數學課很認真的原因！那妳呢，梅爾？妳長大後想做什麼？
梅爾：我想當警察。
傑克：我爸是警察，他說需要記住很多規則，也要很勇敢。
梅爾：我想我做得到。我真的想幫助守護人民的安全。

Dialogue

 18 P. 52

A：你離開學校後想要做什麼？
B：我不確定。
A：你最喜歡做什麼事呢？
B：我喜歡幫助人。
A：那當醫生如何？或可能護士咧？
B：當醫生聽起來很酷，但得很了解人體才行。
A：沒問題的，你努力的話，我相信你能學會的！

Unit 10 What's the Weather Like in Your Country? 你國家的天氣怎麼樣？

Warm Up

 P. 54

1 sunny 2 snowy 3 rainy 4 windy
5 hot 6 cold 7 cool 8 warm

Speak & Listen

 19 P. 56

1 a 2 d 3 a 4 b

Mei: Bobby, you're from Italy, right?
Bobby: Yes, I am. Why do you ask?
Mei: I want to go there on vacation. What's the best time to visit?
Bobby: I think spring is the best time to visit. The weather is warm and sunny at that time of year.

Mei:	What about summer? Is the weather in summer good, too?
Bobby:	The weather in summer is sunny, but it's very hot. It's not a nice time to be walking around sightseeing.
Mei:	So spring is better?
Bobby:	Yes, fall is pretty nice, too. It's cool and sunny. Winter is cool but it can be quite rainy.
Mei:	Got it. I'll try to go in spring, then. Thanks, Bobby.
Bobby:	No problem!

玫：　巴比，你是義大利人對嗎？
巴比：是，我是。為何問這個？
玫：　我想去那裡度假。最適合到訪的時間是什麼時候呢？
巴比：我想最適合春天去那。那時是一年之中溫暖晴朗的天氣。
玫：　那夏天呢？夏天天氣也很好嗎？
巴比：夏天陽光普照，但非常熱，不適合到處走動觀光。
玫：　所以春天比較好囉？
巴比：對，秋天也很不錯，天氣涼爽又有太陽。冬天也涼爽但可能會常下雨。
玫：　了解。那我儘量春天去。謝謝你，巴比。
巴比：不客氣！

Dialogue

20 P. 56

A：嗨，你是英國人，對嗎？
B：是，我是。你為何這樣問？
A：我明年要去那裡度假。
B：喔，太好了！你要什麼時節去？
A：我要春天去。那時的天氣通常是如何呢？
B：挺冷的，而且下很多雨。你應該帶著雨衣和一些保暖的衣服。
A：我會的！謝謝你的建議。

Unit 11 How Will We Get There? 我們要如何到達那裡？

Warm Up

P. 58

1 c　2 a　3 e
4 b　5 d　6 f

Speak & Listen

21 P. 59

1. Abby and Lee are going to the **toy fair** this weekend.
2. Lee's father **can't** take them.
3. In the end they decide to take the **train** because it's **cheaper**.
4. Abby will meet Lee at the **station** at 10 o'clock on **Sunday**.

Abby:	Hey, Lee. Don't forget we're going to the toy fair this weekend.
Lee:	I won't. I'm really looking forward to it. I heard there'll be lots of cool new designs on show there.
Abby:	Is your dad still driving us?
Lee:	Oh, I forgot to tell you. He has to work, so he can't take us.

Abby: Oh, no! So, how will we get there?
Lee: We can take the train or we can take a taxi.
Abby: A taxi will be too expensive. Let's take the train.
Lee: I agree. Taking the train will be cheaper, and it's only a little slower than taking a taxi.
Abby: Great! Then I'll meet you at the train station on Saturday morning at 10 o'clock.
Lee: OK. See you there.

艾比：嘿，李，別忘了我們這週末要去玩具博覽會喔。
李：我不會忘啦，我很期待呢。聽說那邊會展示很多很酷很新的設計。
艾比：你爸還是會載我們去嗎？
李：喔，我忘記告訴妳，他要工作，所以沒辦法載我們了。
艾比：喔不！那我們要怎麼去那？
李：我們可以搭火車或搭計程車。
艾比：計程車太貴了，我們搭火車吧。
李：我同意。搭火車比較便宜，而且也比搭計程車稍微貴一點而已。
艾比：太好了！那我們星期六早上 10 點在火車見囉？
李：好，在那見啦。

Dialogue

A 22 P. 60

A：嘿！你這週末要做什麼？
B：我要去故宮博物館，這是台灣最有名的博物館。你想要來嗎？
A：我想要！我們要怎麼到那？可以用走的嗎？
B：不行，用走的太遠了。我們可以搭巴士或計程車。
A：我們搭巴士吧，比較便宜。
B：太好了。那我星期六早上 9 點半在公車站跟你碰面。
A：好啊！在那碰頭囉。

Unit 12 Good Manners 有禮貌

Warm Up

A P. 62

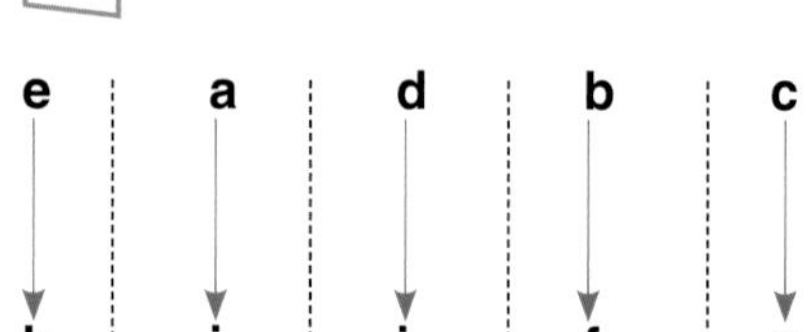

Speak & Listen

B 23 P. 63–64

Rich saw	[ ] a man spitting on the street. [ ] a man cutting in line. [✓] a man throwing trash on the ground.
Rich told the man to	[✓] put it in a trash can. [ ] take it home with him. [ ] leave it on the ground.
The man said	[ ] he dropped it by mistake. [✓] he couldn't find a trash can. [ ] it wasn't his trash.
Rich told the man	[✓] where he could find a trash can. [ ] he would call the police. [ ] he would help him throw away his trash.

Molly: Hi, Rich. Are you OK? You look angry.

Rich: Hi Molly. Yes, I'm angry. I saw a guy on the street throw his empty water bottle on the ground.

Molly: Oh, no. Did you ask him to pick it up?

Rich: Yes, I did. I told him he should put it in a trash can.

Molly: And what did he say?

Rich: He said he couldn't find a trash can.

Molly: But there are trash cans everywhere! I think he was just lazy.

Rich: I agree. I told him there was a trash can at the end of the street.

Molly: So, did he pick his trash up in the end?

Rich: Yes, he did.

Molly: Good. You did the right thing telling him to pick it up.

Rich: Thanks, Molly.

茉莉：嗨，李奇。你還好嗎？你一副生氣的樣子。

李奇：嗨茉莉。對，我在生氣。我在路上看到有個男的往地上丟他的空水瓶。

茉莉：喔，不。你有請他撿起來嗎？

李奇：有，我有，我告訴他，他應該把瓶子放進垃圾桶。

茉莉：那他說什麼？

李奇：他說他找不到垃圾桶。

茉莉：但到處都有垃圾桶啊！我看他是在偷懶吧。

李奇：我同意。我告訴他街道盡頭就有一個垃圾桶。

茉莉：所以，他最後有把他的垃圾撿起來嗎？

李奇：有，他有。

茉莉：太好了。你做得很對，有告訴他要撿起來。

李奇：謝謝妳，茉莉。

Dialogue

 24 P. 64

A：不好意思。

B：怎麼了？

A：請不要丟垃圾在地上，這樣對環境不好。

B：喔，很抱歉，我找不到垃圾桶。

A：這條街道盡頭有一個。

B：好的，我會撿起來並丟進垃圾桶。

A：謝謝你。

Unit 13 A Surprise 驚喜

Warm Up

 P. 66

Joan [**d**]	Jenny [**c**]	Fred [**b**]
Anne [**e**]	Nick [**f**]	Kate [**a**]

Speak & Listen

 25 P. 67

[ ]	[✓]	[ ]	[ ]

Troy: Hey, Gina.

Gina: Hey, Troy.

Troy: Dan's birthday is next week. What should we buy him for his birthday present?

Gina: Hmm. Good question. I know he likes baseball. How about we buy him a ticket to a baseball game?

Troy: That's a good idea. But I think baseball tickets are quite expensive.

Gina: Yes, you're right. Hey! I know. Why don't we buy him a baseball bat? I know he needs a new one because his old one broke.

Troy: Good idea! How much is a baseball bat?

Gina: It's not too expensive. Together we should be able to buy one for him.

Troy: OK. Let's go shopping for one this weekend.

Gina: Great!

特洛伊： 嘿，吉娜。

吉娜： 嘿，特洛伊。

特洛伊： 下禮拜是丹的生日，我們要買什麼給他當生日禮物啊？

吉娜： 恩，問得好。我知道他喜歡棒球，我們買給他棒球賽的門票怎麼樣？

特洛伊： 這主意不錯。但我想棒球門票挺貴的。

吉娜： 對，你說得對。嘿！我知道了。我們何不買給他棒球棒？我知道他需要一根新的，因為他舊的壞了。

特洛伊： 好點子！棒球棒多少錢啊？

吉娜： 沒有很貴。我們一起付的話應該可以買一根給他。

特洛伊： 好啊，那這週末我們去買一根給他。

吉娜： 贊成！

Dialogue

A  26 P. 68

A：麥克生日你要買什麼給他？

B：我要買給他一件足球衣，因為我知道他有多喜歡足球。

A：聽起來是個好禮物。他還喜歡什麼啊？

B：他還喜歡音樂。

A：或許我可以買給他耳機。

B：好主意。我相信他會喜歡的！

Unit 14 What's Cooking? 你在做什麼？

Warm Up

A P. 70

1 B 2 C 3 B 4 C 5 C

6 C 7 B 8 C 9 B 10 B

Speak & Listen

B  27 P. 71

1 F 2 F 3 T 4 T 5 F

Kay: Mmm! What's that smell, Dad?

Dad: I'm baking some muffins.

Kay: Oh yay! I love your homemade muffins. Are they blueberry flavored?

Dad: No, this time I thought I'd try making lemon muffins.

Kay: I love lemon! How long will it be before they're ready?

Dad: They should be ready in about ten minutes.

Kay: Great! I can't wait to try them!

[Ten minutes later . . .]

Dad: Kay! The muffins are ready.

Kay: Yes! Finally!

Dad: Here, have a taste. What do you think? Are they too sour?

Kay: No, they're just right. A little sour and a little sweet. Dad, they're delicious!

Dad: I'm glad you like them! If you want, you can take some to school tomorrow to share with your friends.

Kay: That would be great! Thanks, Dad!

凱： 恩！這是什麼味道啊，爸？

父親： 我在烤馬芬。

凱： 喔耶！我愛你烤的馬芬。是藍莓口味的嗎？

父親： 不是，我想說這次來烤烤看檸檬馬芬。

凱： 我愛檸檬！還要多久才會好？

父親： 大概十分鐘後會好。

凱： 好！我等不及要吃啦！

〔10 分鐘後〕

父親： 凱，馬芬好囉！

凱： 太棒了！終於！

父親： 來嚐嚐看。妳覺得如何？會太酸嗎？

凱： 不會，剛剛好，酸酸甜甜。爸，很好吃耶！

父親： 很高興妳喜歡！妳想要的話，可以明天帶一些去學校跟妳的朋友分享。

凱： 那就太好了！謝謝你，爸。

Dialogue

A

 28 P. 72

A：你在做什麼啊？

B：我在烤布朗尼。

A：喔！什麼口味的？

B：花生醬與香蕉。

A：我的最愛！還要多久會烤好？

B：大概五分鐘。

A：太棒了！我等不及要嚐一個了。

〔稍後……〕

B：烤好了！

A：哇！看起來好棒喔！

B：你覺得如何？太甜嗎？

A：不會，真的很好吃。

Unit 15 What Do You Do After School?

你放學後會做什麼？

Warm Up

A

P. 74

1 h 2 f 3 c 4 d 5 b

6 g 7 a 8 i 9 j 10 e

Speak & Listen

B

 29 P. 76

5:00 p.m.	6:00 p.m.	**7:00 p.m.**	7:30 p.m.
eat dinner	**practice piano**	go on social media	**do homework**

9:00 p.m.	9:30 p.m.	10:00 p.m.
take a shower	**read**	go to bed

Jen: Hi, Tim. You look tired.
Tim: Hi, Jen. Yeah, I was up late last night doing homework.
Jen: You need to organize your time better. I'm always in bed by 10 o'clock.
Tim: I wish I could be in bed so early. What do you do after you get home?
Jen: Well, I have dinner with my family first. Then I practice piano for an hour. After that, I take a break by going on social media.
Tim: How long do you spend on social media?
Jen: Usually around 30 minutes. Then I do my homework. That usually takes me about an hour and a half.
Tim: And after that?
Jen: I take a shower, and then I read until it's time to sleep.
Tim: You really are organized!
Jen: You should try it sometime! Then you'll be less tired in class!

珍：嗨，提姆。你看起來累累的。
提姆：嗨，珍。對啊，我昨晚很晚睡，在寫作業。
珍：你需要好好管理你的時間。我晚上 10 點一定會上床。
提姆：我希望我能早點睡。妳到家後都做些什麼啊？
珍：我先和家人吃晚餐，再練鋼琴一小時，之後我會休息一下，用社交媒體。
提姆：妳在社交媒體上花多少時間？
珍：通常大概 30 分鐘。然後我會寫作業，常常花我大概一個半小時。
提姆：那之後咧？
珍：我洗個澡然後看書，直到該睡覺的時間。
提姆：妳真有條有理耶！
珍：你有時間也該試試！上課時你就不會那麼累了！

Dialogue

30 P. 76

A：你回家後在做什麼？
B：我和家人吃晚餐，然後做家事。
A：那會花你多少時間？
B：大概花我 30 分鐘。
A：在那之後你做什麼？
B：我休息一下，看些漫畫書。
A：你花多少時間做這個？
B：大約一個小時。之後我做功課直到晚上 9 點。
A：你幾點上床睡覺？
B：我每晚通常 10 點前睡覺。

Unit 16 Save the Planet 守護地球

Warm Up

P. 80

1 D 2 E 3 C 4 A 5 B

 P. 80

waste water — turn off the tap when you're brushing your teeth

waste electricity — turn off the lights when you are leaving a room

buy plastic bags — bring your own cloth one

use plastic straws — use a metal one

waste paper — write on both sides

Speak & Listen

B 🎧31 P. 81–82

1 You really shouldn't. . . .	[ ] go everywhere by car. [✓] use paper cups. [ ] waste water.
2 You should use. . . .	[✓] a water bottle. [ ] a plate. [ ] a metal one.
3 If everyone just helps a little, we can. . . .	[ ] stop wasting so much paper. [ ] save a lot of water. [✓] make our planet much cleaner.
4 Thanks for. . . .	[ ] helping the planet. [✓] changing your mind. [ ] being nice.

Rob: Hey, Dora. Are you going to get some water?
Dora: Yes.
Rob: Great. Could you get me some too?
Dora: Sure. Pass me your water bottle.
Rob: Oh, I don't have one. Just use one of the paper cups.
Dora: You know, you really shouldn't use paper cups.
Rob: Why not? What's the problem?
Dora: They're really bad for the environment. You should use a water bottle.
Rob: I don't know. Does it really make a big difference?
Dora: Yes. If everyone just helps a little, we can make our planet much cleaner.
Rob: Hmm. Yeah, I guess you're right. OK, tomorrow I'll be sure to bring my water bottle.
Dora: That's great! Thanks for changing your mind.

羅伯：嘿，朵拉。妳是要去裝水嗎？
朵拉：對。
羅伯：太好了。妳可以也幫我裝一點嗎？
朵拉：好啊。給我你的水壺。
羅伯：喔，我沒有水壺，用紙杯裝就好了。
朵拉：你知道嗎，你真不該使用紙杯的。
羅伯：為何不？有什麼問題嗎？
朵拉：紙杯對環境不好，你應該用水壺。
羅伯：我不知道耶，有差很多嗎？
朵拉：有。如果每個人都貢獻一點心力，我們就能讓我們的地球乾淨一點。
羅伯：恩，對啦，我想妳是對的。好吧，我明天一定會帶我的水壺來。
朵拉：太好了！謝謝你改變想法。

Dialogue

 🎧32 P. 82

A：我們在班上能做什麼事來守護地球呢？
B：我們可以停止浪費紙張。
A：好想法。我們要怎麼辦到呢？
B：我們可以兩面都寫過再丟掉。
C：我同意。我們也可以帶自己的水壺，而不是使用紙杯。
A：好耶！那我們一致同意，就從現在開始做這些事情吧！

英語力 Starter

16堂流利英語聽說入門訓練課

English Now—Starter: Listening and Speaking in Everyday Life

作　　者　Owain Mckimm
翻　　譯　王采翎
英文審訂　Helen Yeh
企劃編輯　葉俞均
編　　輯　王采翎
主　　編　丁宥暄
內文排版　林書玉／執筆者
封面設計　林書玉
製程管理　洪巧玲
發 行 人　黃朝萍
出 版 者　寂天文化事業股份有限公司
電　　話　+886-(0)2-2365-9739
傳　　真　+886-(0)2-2365-9835
網　　址　www.icosmos.com.tw
讀者服務　onlineservice@icosmos.com.tw
出版日期　2024 年 5 月 初版一刷（寂天雲隨身聽 APP 版）

郵撥帳號 1998620-0 寂天文化事業股份有限公司
訂書金額未滿 1000 元，請外加運費 100 元。
【若有破損，請寄回更換，謝謝】

英語力 : 16 堂流利英語聽說入門訓練課 (Starter)(寂天雲隨身聽 APP)/ Owain Mckimm 作 ; 王采翎翻譯 . -- 初版 . -- [臺北市] :
寂天文化 , 2024.04
面；　公分
ISBN 978-626-300-248-7(菊 8K 平裝)
1.CST: 英語 2.CST: 讀本
805.18　113003946